Blood's Angel

Wolfsbane Ridge MC
Book 3

By Author
Marissa Ann

Warning:
Credits:
Cover Design by: Francessca PR & Designs
Editor: Rachel Goldman
Blurb: Melissa Mitchell

ASIN:
ISBN-13: 978-1-7365798-0-0

Prologue

Blood

The first time I ever saw Miranda Grayson was in the parking lot of the grocery store. She had her arms full of grocery bags and was having a hard time opening the trunk of her car.

I walked right up, took the bags, opened her trunk, put everything in and walked away. Without ever saying a single word. I remember looking back before getting on my bike and seeing a look on her face as if she thought I may be missing a few marbles in my head.

Currently; I'd say she was correct in her assessment. I can't seem to put together a complete sentence in her presence. I'm not sure why her presence has that reaction with me. Quite frankly it pisses me off. I'm not always sure if I want to kill something or just fuck her brains out.

Can you fuck someone until you get them out of your system? I'm not really sure but with her, I'd damn sure be willing to try. But I highly suspect after the first taste of her, I'd never let her go.

Since her kidnapping, I'm not too sure she'd ever let another touch her in that way again. Much less a big ass brute like me that can't talk.

Miranda

I've been through hell over this past year but I refuse to allow it to destroy me. They took me from my own home and I am still unsure how exactly they got in. I've not stepped foot back in there since it happened.

Currently I am sharing a room in the Wolfsbane Ridge MC clubhouse with a gorgeous hulk of a man that has rarely spoken two words to me. I should be afraid of him just based on his size. But, oddly, I am comforted by his presence.

I'm sure he'll eventually want me to leave or at least move to a different room. Surely a man like him has a ton of women or maybe even a girlfriend. He wouldn't want to continue to take care of a woman like me. One that is so used up and completely broken.

Uncle John has been by several times already trying to get me to go back home with him. But I am not ready. Especially since he told me that Ray has been by looking for me.

I need to wait until I am stronger. That way I can run because I know if Ray catches me this time, he'll kill me.

Chapter 1

Blood

It's been nearly two weeks since I carried Miranda out of that warehouse down in New Orleans. She refused all help from anyone else but me. She even freaks out if I try to leave the room while the doctor is here to look her over.

So here I stand in a corner of the room with my back to them as he examines her. On the outside, the damage from being beaten has all but faded. But I am certain that it goes deeper to her soul, something only she will be able to heal completely on her own.

"Well, that should do it. Everything appears to be healing very nicely. You still have plenty of pain medication if the soreness becomes too intense for you." Doctor Ortez comments as he begins to put all his stuff back into his bag.

"I don't like the way it makes my head feel dizzy. Almost like I am drunk." She mumbles back.

"Try taking them when you eat. That way you can sleep right after. There is no need for you to suffer through the pain." He admonishes before looking my way.

"I'll make sure she takes them as she needs." I state loud and clear. It's probably the most words she has heard me speak since we brought her back to Montana.

Sure, I sleep in the room with her. Granted, in the chair that sits in the corner. I rarely ever leave her for longer than it takes to go get her something to eat. But talking is something that neither of us have done or even attempted to do. She stares either out the window or at whatever is on the T.V., while I secretly stare at her from the corner of my eye.

She has fascinated me since the day I first spotted her in that parking lot. It was several weeks before she was taken. She had a sad little smile on her face as she went to her car. But even with the sadness, she was beautiful. Just as she still is now. Although; I don't think she knows it.

"Try to get out of this room some. I understand from Timber that you have refused to even go as far as the kitchen. Hiding in this room will only make things worse for you mentally. Get out; interact with some of the other women. Hell, have a drink! Just don't mix it with your pain pills." He tells her as he heads out the door.

"Take her out for a walk." He tells me as he shuts the door.

I look over at her and state, "I'll let you get dressed while I go see how much longer it'll be before lunch is ready."

"Why do I need to get dressed?" She squeaks back at me.

"Doc said you needed to get out some. Figured we could sit in the kitchen with everyone else today. I'll be back to get you in twenty minutes." I answer as I walk out and shut the door again not giving her a chance to argue about it.

As I get close to the kitchen I can hear the other women as they prepare to set the tables for lunch.

It's good to hear them laughing and having fun. With everything that Mina and Bella went through a while back with being kidnapped and tortured, they deserve the happiness they have finally found with my club brothers.

"Hey, Blood, we just saw Doc Ortez leaving a few minutes ago. How is Miranda today?" Mina asks as I walk into the room.

"He thinks she needs to get out of the room some so I told her we would be eating with everyone else today." I respond trying not to sound like a grumbling bear.

"I'll grab an extra plate for her. Has she said much about what she went through?" Bella asks curiously.

"No." I state with a shrug of my shoulders.

"Well, if you are as quiet with her as you are with the rest of us, it's no wonder she hasn't said much. You can be quite intimidating, you know?" Mina states as she fills a bowl with potato salad.

"How?" I question as I stare at her waiting for an answer.

"How are you intimidating?" she asks looking at me. I just nod my head as an answer and wait to see what she says.

"Really, Blood?" she states as she rolls her eyes giving me a clue this is going to be one of her "talks" that tell you how everything you are currently doing is wrong.

The thing about it is that she is usually right. I think it's hilarious when Timber, my club President, is the one on the receiving end of her talks.

"First off, have you truly looked at yourself in the mirror? You are one of the biggest men I've ever seen. You walk around with a constant scowl on your face; you rarely say more than one word when talking and only if a grunt won't do. And you just said you *told her* to get dressed because she was coming in here to eat instead of *asking* her." She states while looking at me with her hands on her hips like a mother hen. It causes my mouth to twitch wanting to smile.

"Surely I'm not missing Blood finally getting one of your talks baby." Timber states as he walks into the room, stopping to kiss Mina.

"She makes me sound like a bear." I growl as I turn to leave to go get Miranda from her room.

"Because you are a bear!" Mina yells out amid Timber's laughter at my expense.

Miranda

He left me staring at the door he closed behind him as he left. The man barely talks but there are times that I catch him looking at me as if he's looking at something rare that scares him. There's no way that I scare a big bear of a man like him.

He's huge with broad shoulders, at least six and a half feet tall and huge muscled arms bigger than my whole body. He looks more like a man that should be in a body builder magazine.

It doesn't take me long to get dressed. I'm not actually afraid to go out into the clubhouse. I just don't know who I can trust. Someone in this club may know Ray and give him a way to get to me.

I am fairly sure that when he lost access to my bank account, he used me as leverage to get more money. Maybe even went so far as to sell me to those traffickers for the money he needed to afford his drug problem. I'm just unsure of how to prove it.

I should have walked away from the relationship the very first time he hit me. But I didn't. I became one of those women that made excuses for him and believed the lie that it would never happen again. But it did happen again and progressively got worse to the point that the abuse was almost daily.

He controlled where I went, who I talked to and even how I dressed. If I wore something that wasn't approved by him first, the beating I received would be brutal. He never hit my face though. Only ever hitting me in areas that would be covered easily by my clothes.

Ray liked my face to be flawless as he loved to flaunt me in front of those he called his business associates. What I didn't find out until later was that he planned to "loan" me out to these men in exchange for favors and money.

I thought locking him out of my house and my life would save me from any more of the bullshit I had gone through. But it didn't. I'm almost certain he sent his associates after me anyway.

I put too much stock in the thought that Ray knowing my Uncle was a cop would get him to disappear. Instead, he tried to make me disappear. Knowing I had a cop in the family didn't stop the abuse either. God I was stupid!

I've avoided telling my Uncle any of this so far. I was ashamed to let him know what kind of a mess I had truly let my life turn into. I do need to tell him soon. Get the authorities involved somehow. I just want to go back to having a normal boring life.

I'm sitting on the edge of the bed still thinking about everything I have been through when the door opens and Blood walks in the room.

He just stands there looking at me as he holds the door open. I guess that is his way of letting me know it's time to go to lunch so I get up and walk out in front of him. As we get closer to the voices I hear talking, my steps become slower until I feel Blood walking right next to me.

"You'll be okay." He whispers to me as I feel him take my hand into his large one.

A tingling feeling runs up my arm and I wonder if he can feel it too. It's so odd to me, that I feel so comfortable around him.

When the nightmares come to me in the middle of the night, he's right there to quiet my fears. He never mentions them the next morning and I am unwilling to really talk about them out loud just yet.

I know I probably need to. I am afraid to say out loud what all I went through. It might give it more power over me than it already has.

We walk into the room that has several tables setup with food and several people walking around filling plates. They all look our way as we walk in causing nervousness in my stomach.

"I am so glad you could join us today! Come right over here, you and Blood can sit with us." I smile at Mina as she speaks and motions toward a table that I can see Timber, Blade and Bella already sitting at.

I had met several of the members in New Orleans before we left but the women I met were truly there for me at the time. Not being able to really move to wash your own hair sucks, but it sucks less when two strangers with big hearts take care of you like a long lost sister.

As I sit down, I notice that Bella has their baby with them and I smile in her direction. I'm surprised when Blood seems to fill my plate while I am distracted by the baby for a few minutes.

"I can't eat all of this." I whisper to him but all he does is grunt at me.

"If you'll poke him in the eye, I bet he'd give you more than just a grunt." murmurs Mina from across from me.

I just give her a small smile as I begin to eat the food in front of me. I become so lost in my own thoughts for so long that by the time I look down again, I have managed to eat everything on my plate. Guess I was hungrier than I thought, I think to myself as I sit quietly listening to the conversations around me.

Blood doesn't seem to join into any of the conversations other than a few words here or there. I guess it's good to know that he's this quiet with everyone and not just me.

I notice a tattoo on his arm that draws my attention. It's the same one that I noticed that day he helped me in the parking lot many months ago. I remember thinking it looked sexy as hell and I wanted to follow it up his arm and everywhere else it made lead to.

I'm so distracted by watching the way the tattoo moves on his huge arm when he moves that when the door slams open with a huge bang, my world goes black as the memories take over my mind.

Chapter 2

Blood

"What the fuck happened?" asked Fang while I checked on Miranda who passed out and hit the floor after letting out a piercing scream.

All I can do is look in his direction because I don't know how to answer that question either. We were all sitting at the table eating and talking when she went screaming.

"I think the loud noise you made with the door had a lot to do with it." Bella answers as she presses a cold washcloth to Miranda's forehead. Her answer of course causes me to shoot daggers at Fang with my eyes.

"Fucking hell, Blood, It's not like I meant to!" whines Fang at the thought that I may be pissed off.

I just grunt at him as I pick her up off the floor and head towards my room. The doctor should be coming back soon to check on her. I know that is the first call Timber would have made without me having to ask him to.

That is the type of family we are. We know what each of us need, sometimes before the other even knows it and we get it done.

It's what first drew me to MC life after high school. I had shit parents, they are still shit parents. The only good thing that came from those two miserable human beings was my little sister.

She was always a beautiful little thing and now that she is grown, I have a hard time thinking of her as anything but a little girl. I'm trying, I really am but she tends to attract the wrong kind of men into her life. The kind that makes me want to paint walls with their blood.

The one she recently broke up with learned fast that hitting my sister will get you broken bones. Mother fuckers that hit women disgust me to my core.

Miranda stirs as I lay her down on my huge bed. I watch as her eyes slowly open and she comes to the realization that I have not let her completely go yet.

"There's my Angel." I whisper as her eyes meet mine with confusion.

"What happened?" She questions as she pulls the rest of the way out of my arms.

"You got a little spooked by the sound of the door." Mina answers as she walks into the room with the doctor. "Blood, would you like to step out for a few minutes? Timber said he had some things to run by you." She throws my way without looking at me.

"Be back shortly." I tell no one in particular although I mean it more for Miranda as I walk out the door in search of my President.

Miranda

"Hey there, I am glad to see that you woke up before I actually got here. They tell me you reacted badly to a loud noise. Is that right?" The doctor asks from the side of my bed.

"I think so. I don't really remember." Is the only answer I can give and I watch as he turns to look at Mina.

"Fang walked through the door which banged open from the crazy wind we are getting today. She jumped a mile in her chair, screamed the ceiling down and promptly passed out into the floor. Blood tried to catch her in time but you know how big he is. He couldn't get turned around in the chair before she hit the floor." She states with a small smile from her memory of him.

Her story and the thought of him trying to move quickly in that little chair even puts a smile on my own face. The man is seriously huge.

"Go ahead; you can laugh at the image. I would have laughed like crazy if I hadn't been worried about whether you had hit your head or not." I can tell she is serious which makes me like her even more. Hell, the old me would have laughed too.

We just stare at each other for a minute and before I know it, we are both doubled over laughing. I laugh so hard though that after a minute, it turns into sobs that I just can't seem to stop. Mina just sits next to me and gently rubs my back. The doctor just sits there quietly until I begin to calm down a good bit.

"Miranda dear," the Doctor states, "I think we need to go ahead and set you up for therapy sessions. I really do think that it will help you. Your reaction to a loud noise suggests possible PTSD from the trauma you went through during your kidnapping. I'm also going to guess that this is the first time you have truly cried since being here. Is it okay with you if we make you an appointment?"

"Do you really think that is necessary? It was just this once?"

"Miranda sweetie, we have all heard the nightmares. You need someone that can help you to learn how to cope with all that you have been through." Mina comments from beside me.

"Can it be a woman doctor please? No offense."

"None taken dear. I have known since that first day that you are experiencing issues with men being around. With the exception of Blood, of course." He says with a smile my way. "Mina, I will forward the information your way by this afternoon." He mentions as he prepares to leave.

Blood

"Hey Prez, Mina said you needed to talk to me?" I question as I walk into the office at the shop. All the guys are back at work this morning preparing a new custom build for some rich fuck that likes to pretend to be a biker on the weekends.

"Yeah man, come on in and shut the door."

I do as he asks and plop down onto the sofa he has in the room. The chair in front of his desk is way too small for my huge ass. I broke the last one he had in here, so I am not going to attempt to sit in this new one.

"This girl you've attached yourself to has got baggage. She is going to need therapy and a lot of other shit. You realize this, yeah?" His comments immediately piss me off.

"If you don't want her here, just say so. We'll go somewhere else. Really I am surprised at you. I never took you to be so fucking cold about women." I growl at him as I start to stand up to leave.

"Now hold on! That is not what the fuck I meant! You have attached yourself to this woman and as far as I know, you barely fucking know her! As for her needing help, I am completely all in to make sure she gets everything she needs. Including getting back to the real world. Even if that means leaving you behind!"

I realize when he finishes that I jumped to conclusions. He wants to make sure of my intentions toward her. Protecting her. But also worried about me, his club brother.

"She and I do barely know each other. I saw her months ago for the first time. At the grocery store. It was like lightning hit my chest. I haven't been able to get her out of my mind since that day.

When Officer Wilson showed up because of his missing niece with a picture of her, I recognized her. I knew I'd do anything to get her back. It's why I pushed you so hard about letting me go to New Orleans. I don't know how to explain it, but all I can say is that I currently feel like she is extremely important to me." I explain as best I can.

He probably thinks I am a huge dumbass because seriously, the shit doesn't make any fucking sense to me either.

"Hey, Prez, don't mean to interrupt but you're needed at the front gate before Fang kills some dickhead that is demanding we let him inside." Dane says as he sticks his head through the door into the office.

"We'll be right there." Timber comments on a sigh, as he waits for Dane to close the door again before continuing our conversation.

"If you feel as though this girl is important to you, Blood, then she is important to the entire club. We will all help her to get through the hell that her kidnapping put her through. And from what happened earlier I'm going to say she has a hard battle ahead of her on her road to recovery. You also need to realize that she very well may not feel the same feelings for you that you are feeling towards her. If that winds up being the case and she wants to leave, we will all help her to get set up in a new place if she chooses. Understand?"

"Yeah, Thanks Prez. That is all I can ask of you. I appreciate it." Is the only comment I can manage without looking like a pussy in front of my club brother.

"Now, let's go see what the fuss is at the front gate. God forbid this club have an entire fucking day without a ton of shit happening." He gripes as we walk towards the door causing me to laugh at the disgruntled sound of his voice.

As we get closer to the front gate, we can hear a man demanding he be let inside and issuing all kinds of threats if he isn't.

"What the fuck is going on out here?" Timber's demand seems to cause the jackass to shut up long enough to notice we have walked up.

"I need to go inside!" the piss ant demands.

As Timber talks to the idiot about why he thinks he needs into our club, I take the time to size his ass up. He's dressed nice, business suit, hair slicked back. He gives off the impression of money but a closer look if you know what you are looking at will reveal that it's all for show. When I hear Miranda's name, I tune back into the conversation.

"Who the fuck is Miranda to you?" Timber asks as though bored.

"She's mine and I demand you bring that bitch out here so that I can take her home where she fucking belongs!" As soon as those words are out of his mouth, I want to tear him apart. There's no way my angel is engaged.

"No. Now get the fuck off my property before we remove you ourselves." Growls Timber in a tone we all know not to cross but it appears that the fuckwad isn't recognizing the danger he currently is in.

When all the club brothers, including myself start closing in on him, he seems to come to his senses.

"Alright, alright! But you tell that bitch that she can't hide from me forever." Is his parting shot before he jumps into his car, speeding away.

"Just who the fuck was that?" I ask, directing my question to Fang since he was manning the gate.

"Fucker never said his name." He murmurs staring in the direction the car went.

"Snake?" Timber called out.

"On it!" Was his answer from behind us. I hadn't realized until then that all the club brothers had joined us.

Miranda

Mina had stayed with me after the doctor left. She never tried to push me to talk about the memories of what I had been through. All she had said was that she would be there when or if I was ever ready. I appreciated that more than she could ever know.

I thought Blood would come back as soon as the doctor had left. The doctor had been gone for quite awhile but I still had yet to see him. He had never left me for that long of a time. It was starting to make me feel antsy. For some reason I was more attached to him than I had a right to be.

Mina was just leaving when Blood finally walked back in the door. He always looks broody but when he came in, he looked even more so. He didn't say a word. Not like I really expected him to anyway.

After an hour of watching the T.V. he finally broke the silence that we both are usually very comfortable with.

"What did the doctor have to say?" he groused from his chair in the corner.

"He wants me to see a therapist. Says he'll send the information to Mina later today." I explain as he just shakes his head in agreement.

"Officer Wilson said he'd be here later today to check in on you. He asked if there was anything you want him to pick up from your house for you."

"Could you ask him to get my computer and my backpack? They both should be in my bedroom by the bed." I ask as he takes his phone from his pocket and starts texting on it. A few seconds later it dings with a response.

"He'll bring them with him."

"Thank you. You don't have to sit here with me all day if there is something else you need to be doing. I'll be alright."

"I do need to be in the shop helping today."

"Then, go. I'm fine. I promise. Plus I know where the girls are. Maybe I'll go hang out with them some."

"I'll be back to check on you in a little bit." He says just before bending down and kissing the top of my head.

Although it was a truly innocent touch, one that could have been for a sister, it felt very good to me. Something I haven't felt in a long time. Making me feel truly special and that was something to be scared of.

Chapter 3

Blood

It felt good getting my hands dirty with grease. I love working on engines. Keeping my hands busy doesn't keep my mind from wandering about who that guy was this morning though.

If Miranda was in a relationship, surely she would have mentioned him by now. Even Officer Wilson hasn't mentioned her having anyone else in her life. So, who the fuck was he?

I'm just finishing up to take a break to go check on Miranda when I see Snake walk into Timber's office. A few minutes later, he is motioning for me to come in there too.

"Figured you'd want to know what Snake found on the guy who was looking for Miranda earlier." Timber comments as soon as I walk in.

I turn towards Snake waiting for him to start talking. I've nearly driven myself crazy worrying over this guy having some type of claim on my sweet angel. The way he so easily called her names tells me he certainly doesn't deserve a girl like her.

"His name is Raymond Stein, aka Ray to his friends. His name has been linked to some major players of the Mafia family in New Orleans.

That family is the exact same one suspected of having a huge part in the sex trafficking ring we just helped to bust up." Snake explains to Timber and I.

"The Marcus family." Timber states firmly.

"The very one. Raymond owns a local car dealership on the other side of town. A search of his records that I got into through his computer system at the dealership, lists Miranda as an employee there earlier this year. It's very possible she knows something she shouldn't about his dealings with the Mafia." Snake says with all seriousness.

"This could get ugly." Timber sighs, pinching the bridge of his nose. "Blood, I need you to find out just how close Miranda is to this guy so we can assess just what kind of threat we are looking at here."

I just grunt as I head toward the door. It doesn't really matter to me how close she is to him. He's never getting her back, not even if he's her husband.

Miranda

I ventured out to the kitchen where Mina said she would be working on her latest book release. Bella was at the stove warming up a bottle for Baby Justice when I walked in.

Both have talked to me as if I have always been a part of their little family. Like old friends sharing the gossip from around town.

They shared with me about their own recent trauma with the traffickers that had taken me. While we each went through different things, we all went through hell and are still here. Having these two strong women in my corner will be amazing.

What I have been through will not break me. I will make certain of that. I realize that certain fears may stick with me forever but I will not let it stop my entire life.

Both women have been explaining to me about the "yotes" who are apparently the club girls that are here to share themselves as they see fit. None are made to do anything they don't want to do. I was glad to hear it since knowing what it's like to be hurt in such a way.

"Do these girls help Blood with anything?" Is the question that slips out of my mouth before I can stop it. The thought of Blood being with anyone sends a painful hitch through my chest.

"Blood tends to look frightening so I highly doubt he's been with any of them." Bella smiles in my direction causing my face to turn red because she knew why I was asking.

"Any of who?" Is the growling voice we all hear from the doorway. A voice that causes butterflies in my stomach but is currently making me want to fall through the floor from getting caught asking about his sex life.

"This is an A and B conversation between us girls, Blood, so C your way back out the door." States Mina very seriously.

Looking at Blood to gage his reaction to Mina who spoke so sarcastically at him, shows a small twitch at the corner of his mouth. He never lets the smile come all the way out however. He just grunts at the three of us as he turns around, headed back outside.

As soon as we hear the door shut behind him, Bella and Mina both double over laughing. I am not sure how to react myself. Blood is huge. If he were to ever get truly mad, he could break all my bones with one arm.

"Are you two not afraid of him?" I ask them both seriously.

"The better question here Miranda is if you are afraid of him. Are you?" Bella asks as she rocks the baby in her arms.

I think it over for only a few seconds but already know the answer. I'm not afraid of him. He's like a huge gentle giant with a big heart that he hides behind that constant scowl on his beautifully handsome face.

"No. No I'm really not." I state as a smile spreads across my own face.

Blood

"Did you ask her?" Is the question I get from Timber when I walk back into the shop.

"I will later. She was actually not in the bedroom when I went to check on her. She's in the kitchen with the two smart mouths, Mina and Bella, talking and laughing. I didn't want to disrupt that for her."

"Our women giving you a hard time again?" Blade remarks as he walks up.

I give my usual grunted reply as I go back to working on the sportster in front of me. By the end of the day, I'm covered in sweat, dirt and grease.

At least the sportster I was working on for a local customer can be picked up tomorrow. It feels good to get back to work after being so idle since getting back from New Orleans.

I don't regret all the time I have spent in Miranda's company. Despite not really talking, I have learned a great deal about her.

For instance, she loves French vanilla creamer in her coffee. A lot of it. She also gets a slight pink to her cheeks the few times she caught me flat out staring at her. Thoughts of her cheeks remind me of just how soft her skin is which causes my pants to feel too tight behind my zipper

Wanting to get in the shower before I am caught sporting a hard on, I head straight to the bedroom. I realize as soon as I walk in that Miranda is still with Mina so I grab some clean clothes and close myself into the bathroom.

Stripping quickly, I step into the shower as I turn the water on. It's cold at first but maybe it'll help relieve my hard cock. I lean my head against the wall as the water washes over me, easing the muscles in my back.

Not realizing which bath wash I have grabbed, I lather my body. Then the smell of Miranda hits my face and my cock that had deflated now springs back to life with a vengeance.

I continue washing with her soap anyway, eventually running my soapy hand along my engorged cock making myself moan. I've not had a woman in months.

Knowing Miranda is still gone from the room, I continue to stroke myself. I imagine sinking deep into her hot body as I suck her breasts. It only takes a few strokes with that mental image before I cum all over the wall in front of me.

That's when I hear the gasp at the door causing me to look in that direction. I barely see Miranda as she quickly closes the door. Fuck. I should have made sure the door was locked.

Just my luck she catches me jerking off. I hope like hell I didn't scare her. That's the only thoughts I have as I get out to dry off and get dressed.

Miranda

Oh God, why did I go in there? I could clearly hear the shower running so it's not like I can say I didn't know he was in there.

What is wrong with me? Because I am fairly certain that if I had caught him earlier than right when he came, I would have kept watching until the end.

How could I want a man physically after the abuse I have been through? I definitely wanted him if my panties being wet were anything to judge by.

I wasn't even certain if I could be touched in that way without freaking the hell out. I'm going to make sure Mina sets up that therapy appointment for me first thing tomorrow. It's time I learn how to cope with these issues and hopefully move on with my life.

I'm still thinking over everything when Blood comes out of the bedroom. I notice he smells exactly like my body wash but I don't comment on it.

"There's something I need to ask you about before we head to dinner." He says, as he leans against the dresser.

"Sure."

"Who is Raymond Stein?" Of all the questions he could have asked, that one was not what I expected.

"Why are you asking about him? Did he find me?" I gulped.

"There's no reason for you to be afraid. No one will bother you here. You're safe. I would never allow you to be hurt again." Blood whispers as he cautiously walks closer to me.

"He's a very bad man Blood."

"Can you talk to me about him sweet Angel?"

"Why do you call me that?" I demand.

"Because the first time I ever laid eyes on you in that parking lot, I thought you looked like a sad beautiful Angel." He states matter of factly.

We both move to the bed to sit down. Although I am nervous, I am not afraid of him.

"I met Ray about a year before I was taken. He hired me as his bookkeeper at the car dealership. He was nice at first. Took me out on several dates. Then one day I found inconsistencies in the financial statements. When I asked about them, I was told to leave it alone.

After that, I felt as if I couldn't work there any more. So I quit. Ray however wasn't willing to just let me go. He thought we had something more than we actually did." At this point in my story, I start to feel as if I can't breathe so I stop talking altogether. Looking wildly about the room, I'm ready to bolt for the door when he grabs both of my hands waiting for me to look into his eyes.

"It's okay Angel. That's enough for now." Blood murmurs, pulling me closer to lay my head on his shoulder.

Blood

A little after one in the morning, a soft moan coming from the bed wakes me from my usual spot in the corner of the room. Looking over at her sleeping form in my giant bed I can see that this is not her usual nightmare. She is most certainly dreaming though.

Getting up from the chair, I quietly make my way over to the bed. Lying next to her, I gently pull her closer until she is nestled into my side.

I watch as her eyelids flutter open, staring straight into my eyes that are now only a few inches away. She never says a word. Just closes her eyes once more before drifting off to sleep again.

I continue to lay awake, holding her close and rubbing small circles on her back for over an hour. I still don't understand the connection that I feel to her.

Is this what love is? Does it just sneak up and hit you one day? That day in the parking lot, it was as if my soul said *this is her.* I haven't been the same since. What if she could never feel the same for me?

Chapter 4

Miranda

I've gone to several therapy appointments over the past week that Mina has made sure that I've attended. Blood has been busy working in the shop with the rest of the guys, so hanging out with the girls has become something that I look forward to.

The first day I ventured out with Mina to attend my appointment, I only had three panic attacks. After the second one before ever getting to the doctors office, Mina had asked if I wanted to just go back to the clubhouse.

I wouldn't let her take me back though. I am stronger than that and I'll keep reminding myself of it until I don't have to any more.

"What are you in such deep thought about over there?" Mina questions as she continues to type away on her computer.

"I was just wondering if there is a place close by that teaches self defense."

"There's a new place that just opened in that new shopping center on the other side of town." Bella pipes in from her place at the oven as she waits for the brownies to get done.

"What new place?" Mina and I ask at the same time which causes us both to chuckle.

"It's called Hays Den. It just opened last week. I read on the flyer that they just opened and are offering memberships at a discount for a limited time." she answers as she takes the brownies out, setting them on top of the stove to cool a little bit.

"Hays Den? What kind of name is that?" Mina murmurs as she looks up from her work.

"I think it's a cool name really. Besides, the girl that owns it is named Hayden. She's been into the coffee shop a few times. My mom said she is a really sweet person." Bella continues as she comes to sit at the table.

"Think we could go check it out tomorrow after my appointment?" I direct my question to Mina.

"Sure. I will need to mention it to the guys though. They like to check out any place we girls in the club may frequent often. You can't ever be too careful." She answers as she looks over at Bella.

I've noticed since being here that all the men in the club care very much for all the women. They all take special care even though they themselves don't have an ol' lady. Always respectful, even to the yotes that are considered the club girls.

Blood

The girls just left a few minutes ago headed to Miranda's next appointment and apparently to Hays Den to check out the self defense class that is offered there.

"Why didn't anyone tell me that the girls were looking for a self defense class? What do we know about this Hays Den, anyway?" I demand from the doorway leading into Timber's office. Apparently, I also interrupted a phone call by the looks of it.

"Don't you know how to knock?" he grumbles as he hangs up the phone.

"I never have before." I retort.

"Your ass used to be quieter too. Rarely talking."

"Well? What about Hays Den?" I persist causing Timber to roll his eyes at me.

"It's a new workout place that was recently opened by a young woman named Hayden Lynn. She's a single mom, stays to herself and has a clean record. Anything else you want to know?" He raises his brow.

I just give my usual grunt as I begin to leave his office. Before I can shut the door he reminds me that church is in less than an hour and to not be late.

He knows me well enough to know that if I start work on a new project in the shop I am likely to forget to watch the time.

I go back to my own workstation to go over the work orders that need to be done before the end of the week. That at least will keep me from losing track of time.

Miranda

I had a really good session with my therapist today. She said that there was nothing wrong with my attraction to Blood.

In fact she encouraged me to engage more with him. That it would help to pull me back from the darkness that sometimes takes over my body from the trauma that I have suffered.

I hate that I might have a panic attack at every little sound. That I sometimes flinch just from someone moving too fast around me. I especially hate the nightmares at night although those are what currently brings Blood to the bed and his strong arms that hold me for the rest of the night.

I'm still remembering those strong arms as we walk across the parking lot towards the door to Hays Den.

I'm so deep into my thoughts; I don't realize that someone is behind me until they grab my arm. Immediately I scream getting the attention of Mina and Bella at the same time.

All I can see is Mina brandishing a gun, pointed directly at whoever has grabbed me. I'm almost too stunned to speak.

"What?" I squeak before looking over at the face of the man who still has a hold of my arm. I instantly recognize my Uncle. Apparently at the same time that Mina realizes it is him as well.

"Sorry Officer Wilson." She coolly says as she puts the gun back into her purse.

"You could have killed me young lady!" Uncle John admonishes.

"Highly unlikely as the safety was on and my finger wasn't even on the trigger. Besides, you shouldn't sneak up on any of us that way, especially Miranda." She admonishes.

"I just wanted to say hi for a minute and check on you baby girl. I didn't mean to scare you." He turns his eyes my way, looking a little sad.

"I'm doing a lot better Uncle John. We are actually headed into Hays Den to see about self defense classes." I smile at him, most likely for the first time since I was brought back.

"Good. I miss my sweet independent niece that had no problems giving me a swift kick in the ass when I needed it. So, does this mean you are ready to at least move to my house so that I can take care of you? I've missed you." he smiles back.

"I don't think that I am ready for that just yet Uncle John." I reply as my heart rate kicks up at the thought of Blood not being there.

"We have a family cookout every Saturday if you'd like to join us. I'm sure Miranda would enjoy more time with you if you'd like to come by." Mina informs him as we reach the door.

"Sure. I can come Saturday."

"That will be great. We will see you then." We all say our goodbyes as we walk into the Hays Den.

At the front counter we ask for the manager and are directed to have a seat while we wait. A few minutes later, a woman in her early twenties comes from the back with a little girl around four years old. She sends the child into another room before walking in our direction.

"I'm the owner, Hayden Lynn, may I help you?" introducing herself to us.

"I'm Mina, this is Bella and Miranda. We wanted to see about signing up for your self defense classes. Do you teach them yourself?"

"Yes, I teach the women's class although I do have a male helper at every class as I think it is important to work with typical male assailants. It's harder for women who are so much smaller than a man to get away or defend herself."

"When are the classes?" I ask as I now really want to be signed up for the next one.

"We have a class every Monday and Wednesday night. You can do one class per month or all of them. That is up to you. Let me get you all a price list and sign up sheet. That way you can think about it, then let us know," she explains as she reaches behind the front counter.

As she does so, that small child that was with her earlier comes running up and wraps herself around Hayden's leg.

"Hey, now, you know you are supposed to be in my office watching cartoons." Hayden whispers to her. "This is my daughter, Hanley. She's not normally running around here but my sitter needed today off for an appointment."

"No worries. We love kids." Mina comments as she takes the papers from Hayden.

"We'll let you know by Monday night. It was really nice to meet you Miss Lynn."

"Call me Hayden, please." She smiles as she walks us to the door.

While I think about how excited I am for the classes, I can't help but be a little apprehensive about working with a man that close.

Blood

Saturday night, long after the family gathering, the clubhouse starts to get loud and rowdy like it usually does. Miranda having learned from the other girls what can transpire on the weekends went to the room hours ago. Leaving me to drink with the boys.

I never partake in the craziness like some of the other unattached brothers do. Mostly because I want to be sure I don't catch something that could make my cock fall off. It still surprises me though when the girls try.

We have club girls, all of which willingly give themselves to any club brother that looks in their direction. On the weekends though, we also get some of the local girls and women that are just out looking for a fast thrill.

Tonight, one in particular has been trying to get my attention. Maybe I am more drunk than usual because I am considering taking her up on her offer.

Right as I am about to head over in her direction, we hear a scream coming from the hallway leading to the bedrooms. I take off at a dead run knowing that it is my Angel.

As I storm into the room, I can see Miranda lying on the bed with frightened eyes. I shut the door behind me, locking out all those who had also followed the scream and approached the bed slowly.

"Angel, what is it? Are you okay?" I murmur as I slowly sit on the edge next to her. She finally seems to shake loose from the trance-like state she was in just moments ago as she moves closer to me.

"It was a dream. Just a dream." I barely hear her as she buries her head into my shoulder. "Please don't leave me."

I get her back into the bed, pull the covers over her and lean back against the headboard beside her.

"I could never leave you." is my whispered words to her as her breathing evens out and sleep claims her once more.

I wake to my head pounding and my cock becoming hard as stone as a warm round ass wiggles against me. I'm not yet fully awake when I push my hardness against her before I realize who I am pushing against.

Hoping to not wake her, I slip out of the bed and head to the shower locking the door behind me this time.

Maybe cold water will help my raging hard-on. I am no longer certain how much more of this my cock can take without having her. But I don't want her to be afraid of me.

Miranda

Blood has been avoiding me and it is starting to piss me off. Sure he's there to make sure I don't need anything. He makes sure I get my medicine; he makes sure I eat but he hasn't spent any long amounts of time with me since we got up on Sunday.

I want to talk to him. Even in our quiet times, we still talked a little bit. I miss it and I feel like a big baby for missing it. It's only Monday afternoon. Maybe he just had things to do. At least that is what I keep telling myself.

Mina, Bella and I are back at Hays Den signing up for the self defense classes she is offering. Timber wouldn't let us come unless we agreed to let one of the prospects go with us. Mina of course argued with him about it at first but finally relented so we wouldn't be late for the first class.

Hayden gives a fast glance over at Dane, the prospect and our guard for the day, who goes to stand by the door as we prepare for class. A tall guy walks in, joining Hayden at the front of the class.

"Okay, let's start. Everyone ready?" Hayden announces.

Two hours later, class is over. Today was pretty easy as she showed us how to throw a punch correctly. It didn't surprise me that Mina already had it down pat without needing to be shown. She had already told me that she had taken classes several years ago.

As we all are walking out, I hear my name being called and turn to look in that direction. Before I am fully turned around, I hear a popping sound before I am thrown to the ground.

Panic washes over me as I scream, struggling to get away from the body on top of me. My arms are grabbed and pinned to my sides.

I finally start to recognize Mina's voice in my ears as my screaming and struggling slows down enough for me to hear what she is saying.

"Breathe Miranda! Slow deep even breathes!" she shakes me as she talks to me. My heart rate starts to slow down until I have my panic attack under control.

That's when I realize that Dane is the one holding me down and he is currently bleeding from a scratch on his face. I let the blood from the scratch distract me from the fact he still has a hold of me until Mina asks him to let me up.

"I'm sorry." is all I can manage to say.

"Nothing to be sorry for. I need to get you girls back to the clubhouse now. Okay?" he quietly says as he looks in Mina's direction.

Blood

"Blood! They need you at the clubhouse! Now!" Fang yells through the door before running out again.

I can tell it is urgent and my mind immediately goes to the fact that Miranda isn't back yet. Throwing all my tools down, I run towards the clubhouse in search of Timber who meets me at the door.

"What is it? Is it Miranda?" I ask urgently.

"She's fine but something happened. They are on their way back now. Mina has been texting me all the information. Miranda was shot at."

"What the fuck!" roars out of my mouth. "Who the fuck was it?"

"That we don't know yet as I have not talked to Dane. He has been busy driving back and according to Mina, Miranda doesn't actually know what happened. She thinks she had another one of her panic attacks. She never even realized she was being shot at." he explains as we hear the engine of the cage pulling through the gates. "Keep your shit together. No need to make her even more frightened." he whispers to me as the SUV comes to a stop.

Walking over to the back to open the door for the girls, I help Miranda out of the backseat.

"Have a good day?" my facial expression is currently blank, showing no signs that anything is wrong. Although she looks at me as if I have lost my mind.

"And he speaks." she whispers before looking back at me. "It was a good class. Learned how to throw a real punch." The smile lighting up her face gives me hope that she could be happy again.

"Maybe you could show me later? After supper maybe?" hoping she would want to spend a little time with me.

"That would be nice." she smiles as she walks into the clubhouse with the other girls.

"Call Church. Tell everyone to be here in an hour." Timber announces as he follows the girls inside.

Chapter 5
Miranda

Everyone has been acting weird since we got back from our first class at Hays Den. I feel as though I missed something during my panic attack earlier. Everyone seems to be tiptoeing around me.

If I'm ever going to work past everything or at the very least learn to cope, I need everyone around me to stop hiding shit. It's starting to piss me off.

I've been in my room, or Blood's room, for the past hour waiting on him to come back. I've tried to remember exactly what was happening when my freak out happened.

My therapist said it was good for me to try to remember during those events so that I could learn to control my body's response to it. Since I am having issues remembering it, I figured I could go ask Mina. She seems to be the type to tell you the truth if you ask a direct question.

As I walk into the kitchen on my hunt for Mina, I see a few of the club girls sitting around the table. They immediately stop talking as I walk in. Instead of acknowledging them, I turn back around and head towards the back yard hoping to find her sitting around the firepit.

I immediately spot both Mina and Bella sitting on a bench near the fire. They both look like they are deep in conversation. A conversation they stop as soon as I am spotted walking in their direction.

"Hey girl. You doing okay?" Mina asks as Bella excuses herself to go check on baby Justice.

"What happened earlier? And please don't pretend not to know what I mean." I get straight to the point as I sit down next to her.

"What do you remember?" she sighs, turning fully toward me.

"We were walking to the car when I heard my name being called and then it was all so fast. Dane had me down on the ground. I think I scratched up his face." I grimace at the memory.

"You don't remember the loud bang just before that?" she looks at me questioningly.

I think hard for a minute before my eyes go wide at the memory. Holy shit! Someone was shooting at me.

"Oh fuck!" is all I can manage as my throat tightens up.

"Hey, now, it's okay. Stay calm. Just breathe. We don't know for sure if they were shooting at you for sure. They could have been shooting at any one of us."

"What about whoever called my name? That can't be a coincidence."

"We don't know for sure yet Miranda. The guys will figure it all out. You are safe here with us. Blood would never let anything happen to you. He cares too much to allow anything to happen."

Her words push my emotions over the edge as a tear starts down my face. I hope what she said about Blood caring that much for me is true.

—

I am beginning to think I am in love with him. A big caring gorgeous man that I barely know. Hell, I don't even know his real name.

But I do know things about him. Things that are important, like the fact that he is extremely gentle even though he is huge and built like a mountain.

He is comfortable in the silence of a room without getting antsy. He always asks what I like instead of thinking he knows what is best.

Blood

We have been in church for more than an hour going over and over every detail of what happened with Dane.

"So we need to find out if any of the businesses around there would be willing to share their surveillance footage with us. Maybe one of them got a shot of whoever yelled her name. It's got to be the same person as the shooter." I comment to the room although I look in Snake's direction.

"I'll see what I can find on the ones I can tap into from my room but we'll need the prospects to go to the businesses that use the old school equipment." he answers back.

"I'll send them out as soon as we wrap up here." Timber shuffles some papers in front of him indicating he has a lot on his mind.

"Is there something else Prez?" I ask as we all notice his agitation.

"Yeah, I got a phone call earlier today. Wrench is finally heading home. He should be here in two days." hearing the news everyone starts clapping, truly excited to be welcoming back one of our brothers.

Prez dismisses church and everyone files out. I stay behind so that I can talk to Timber.

"Everything okay Prez? You didn't seem too excited about Wrench coming back."

"Don't get me wrong, I think it's about fucking time his ass came home. I'm just worried about him. He didn't sound like himself over the phone. It makes me wonder just what the fuck he seen over there."

"If he has issues because of what being in the military has subjected him to, he'll have all of us to help him through it. We are family and we will deal with it as a family."

"I still can't help but worry. You hear all the stories on the news just like I do about the military guys not being able to cope and committing suicide."

"He's stronger than that Prez."

"I hope you are right." He says as we both head out the door.

I grab a beer from the bar before I search out Miranda. From the window I spot her sitting outside with the girls.

Before I can make it to the door, a girl that I recognize as a local that likes coming here to hook up with the guys, wraps herself around me.

Her perfume overwhelms my nose as she rubs her half exposed tits into my chest. I'm about to push her off of me as I hear the door open. Looking over I look into the eyes of my angel. Her eyes go wide for a second before she lowers them and walks towards the hall leading to the bed room.

It's only after she is completely out of sight that I remember the woman rubbing all over me. I grab her arms, setting her arms length away and walk around her.

She's saying something to my retreating back but I don't hear a word of it. I don't give a shit what she is saying. She's not my angel.

Miranda

I walk straight to the room and into the bathroom, locking the door behind me before the tears start to fall. Honestly, I don't have a claim on Blood so the tears just piss me off which causes more to fall. There's a light tap on the bathroom door before I hear Blood say my name.

"I'll be out in a minute." I manage to say without any hint of tears. I take my time giving myself a chance to clear my eyes of any trace of being upset before I walk out to find him waiting for me.

"That isn't what it looked like." he quietly says from his chair.

"Your private life is none of my business." shrugging my shoulder as I walk over to the dresser to get my jacket since it has gotten cooler outside. Putting it on, I turn around and run into a wall of muscle.

"What if I want it to be your business?" he whispers as I slowly look up into his crystal blue eyes.

We just stare at each other for several minutes before I slowly inch up on my toes giving him a soft sweet kiss on his lips. It sends tingles up my spine and before I can move away, he wraps his arms around me pulling me closer.

He slowly uses the tip of his tongue to lick my bottom lip. As I gasp he takes full advantage to deeply kiss me. It doesn't last nearly as long as I would have liked before he slowly releases me as though afraid of my reaction.

He doesn't say anything else as he goes to sit down on the foot of the bed just watching me.

"Are you okay? I didn't mean to frighten you." he sighs.

"You didn't." I sit down next to him on the bed and tentatively place my hand on his thigh. After a few seconds he covers my hand with his own.

"Do you guys know who shot at us earlier?" I ask changing the subject more to clear my own head.

"We thought you didn't realize what had happened?"

"It took a little bit plus I talked to Mina. She didn't tell me what happened, but just talking it through helped me to remember what was going on before the panic attack started. So, do you know yet?"

"Not yet. Snake is looking through surveillance video to see if anything was picked up. Can you remember who it was that called your name just before?"

"I can't be certain as to whose voice it was. Do you think it could be whoever Ray was working with?"

"It's unlikely as the shooter missed. That's a big indicator that whoever it was wasn't a professional that is normally hired by the mob."

"The mob!!" I squeak out in horror.

"Fuck. I guess you didn't know that part?" I shake my head in reply. "Ray has connections with a mob family named Marcus in New Orleans. We think that whatever it is that he suspects you to know is connected to that."

"I actually suspected it; I just didn't have the proof. I knew in my bones he was the reason I was taken. I have a copy."

"A copy of what?"

"Of his financial records that had the inconsistencies. I still have a copy as well as all his passwords. Although he may have changed those by now."

"Holy shit! Where is the copy? It could possibly help Snake figure out how to deal with Ray." He asks.

"There's a secret compartment on the backside of my bedpost at home. The USB drive is in there. I was planning to use it to trace the money back. To figure out a way I could get him to leave me alone for good."

"You should have already shared this information. If not with me, at least with your Uncle."

"I didn't want to put anyone else in danger."

"We'll be fine Angel." he whispers just before kissing me softly.

"So what will you guys do?"

"I can't tell you that. What I can tell you is that we will be fine and so will you. This entire club will always take care of you."

"You honestly don't plan to tell?" I ask in bewilderment.

"Sometimes there will be things that I say are Club business. That means it is something I can not share, even with you. Mina can explain to you how the club works if you'll ask her. But the reason for club business is to keep you safe."

"I don't see how keeping me in the dark will help keep me safe." I know that I am now starting to sound like a petulant child but I honestly can't stand secrets.

"When are you girls supposed to have your next self defense lesson?" He asks, changing the subject.

"We were planning to go Thursday but Mina said that with what happened Timber may not allow us to go. She said she would ask him about getting Hayden to come here to give us the lesson. Apparently you guys have a workout studio in one of the buildings here on the property."

"Yes we do. It's very state of the art too. Most of us guys use it instead of having to go into town. We have actually discussed hiring a manager to run it and open it to the public for a monthly membership fee."

"That could be a good business plan."

"Yes. It could. Come on. Let's go get something to eat." He says as he grabs my hand to help me stand up.

Blood

After getting Miranda a plate of food, I leave her with the other girls who are all sitting around the fire away from the more noisy part of the clubhouse.

I find Timber in his office along with Snake who is showing him something on a laptop. They both look up as I walk in.

"We found something." Snake says as he pushes the laptop in my direction.

"That's Ray." I growl looking at the video.

"It is. I sent Fang and Dane out to look for him. Soon as they have him, they'll call." Timber comments.

"I need someone to go to Miranda's as well. Apparently she has a copy of the shit head's records as well as his passwords."

"No shit?" Timber exclaims sitting up in his chair.

"Tell me where to find it and I'll go get them." Snake says as he shuts the laptop.

"She said there is a hidden compartment on the back side of one of her bed posts. It'll be in there."

"Get Butcher to go with you." Timber tells him.

"He's probably balls deep in pussy at the moment." Snake snickers as he walks out of the room.

Chapter 6
Blood

It's been a week since Miranda told us about the USB drive. Snake has been working hard to decipher the financials. It seems that Ray was smart enough to at least use code words in place of real names and places.

"I'm not sure what we expect to get from all this information anyway. We are not a large enough club to go after, much less take down, the fucking mafia!" Butcher states his opinion to the room.

"I think we all agree on that Butcher. I am looking at this as a way to know just enough that I might possibly have a meeting with the head of the Marcus family. They will be the ones to get Ray out of the picture and hopefully get that family to not come after Miranda. And if we are lucky, get them to not run their operation in our territory." Timber rubs the bridge of his nose as if it is all giving him a headache.

"And if that doesn't actually work?" I ask quietly.

"Then we will do what needs to be done. Now, before everyone leaves, the weather report is calling for snow, possibly blizzard conditions. Everyone might want to bring in their family and prepare to be here for a few days if it gets as bad as they are saying." He says to us all as we all stand up to leave church.

"Hey Timber, what about Wrench? I thought he was supposed to be here a few days ago?"

"He called, said he got held up with paperwork at the base. He should be here tomorrow. Hopefully he'll make it before the weather gets too out of control."

"I guess I will go find Miranda and see if she or the other girls need anything from town for the next several days."

"That's a good idea. I'll go get Mina and give her a list of what I think we'll need. Although I am sure she'll think of a lot more than me."

"Your girl does love to shop." I laugh out as we both leave the room.

Miranda

I've been busy helping the other girls make sure that everyone has everything they need in their rooms since we got back from the store a few hours ago. The roads were already showing signs of ice as we drove back.

"Looks like it's going to be a pretty good blizzard." Mina says as she chops the onions for the stew we are making for dinner.

"I hate the thought of being cooped up for several days. What about you Miranda?" Bella asks.

"I don't mind. Besides, we can build snowmen. I haven't done that in ages!"

"The thought of snow much less enough for snowmen is still crazy to me." Mina laughs.

"You don't get snow in Mississippi?" I've never thought about other places that possibly don't get snow.

"Not really. We get mostly ice and only get it every few years. It'll look like snow but as soon as you step on it, your feet will fly right out from under you. It's happened to me many times." She says with a smile on her face.

"I hate that we will miss our class though. I am starting to really like it."

"We'll get back to it as soon as the roads are passable again. Hayden sure is a quiet woman. She doesn't give much away about herself." Bella mentions.

"I noticed that too. She's a hard one to get to know but I understand it. We all have our secrets and being new in town you are unsure of whom to be friends with. I got lucky when I moved here. Bella and I hit it off right at the beginning." Mina smiles towards her best friend.

We all had just sat down to eat an hour later when Dane walked in with a woman and child trailing behind them. I immediately recognize Hayden and her daughter.

"Found these two walking down the road. Apparently her car slid off into a ditch." Dane says to Timber as he takes his coat off.

Hayden, oh my goodness. Y'all alright?" Mina asks as she jumps up from the table.

"We are fine. I just waited too long to leave town and head home. I knew better but I honestly thought we would make it." She answers as she takes off her jacket and then helps her young daughter.

"You two are more than welcome here. We will find a place for you two to sleep for the night. Come warm up and have some stew." Mina offers as they all come to the tables to sit down.

"Are you a giant?" The little girl asks Blood as she sits in the chair next to him causing everyone at the table to laugh.

"I'm not a giant! You are just tiny." Blood says to her.

"You sure look like a giant to me!" She comments as everyone starts laughing.

"Hanley, behave!" Her mom admonishes.

"She's fine. Blood needs someone that'll argue with him." Mina smiles as she takes a bite of stew.

Blood

I wake up around three in the morning and lay there quietly listening to see if Miranda is dreaming again. When I don't hear anything, I close my eyes to go back to sleep when I hear her say my name quietly.

"Blood, are you awake?"

"Yes Angel."

"Will you come and hold me please? I can't seem to stay asleep." she asks me in such a smile voice there is no way I could refuse. Not that I want to anyway. I relish any excuse to be able to lay in my bed with her and hold her close.

I slide in next to her as she wiggles her ass closer to me. This is going to play havoc on my cock. I only hope I can control him enough that him getting hard doesn't frighten her.

We lay there in silence so long that I think she has finally drifted back to sleep until I feel her push her ass back into me causing my cock to swell. As he gets bigger, she moves even more. I try not to move at all even though this is absolute torture.

I want so badly to hold her leg up, push her panties to the side and ease into her tight pussy giving us both pleasure until we explode.

I don't say anything to her until I feel her warm hands reach back and cup my balls through my clothes.

"Angel, I'm not sure you are ready for this." I manage to growl out into her ear.

"Please Blood." She moans as she pushes her ass into me again.

"I really don't think you are ready for me just yet my sweet Angel. But I will take care of you." I whisper to her.

I move my hands slowly to her hips as I slide them down her skin, moving her panties down to her thighs as I go. I find her clit with one hand while my other hand finds her slick slit. I slowly push two fingers into her as my other hand begins to rub slow circles on her clit.

She moves in rhythm with my fingers that are pumping into her causing friction between our bodies that feels amazing to my cock. I am close to exploding in my shorts so I pump my fingers harder and pinch her clit with my other hand. As I feel her wetness close tight on my fingers, my cock explodes.

I don't stop touching her until her breathing smoothes out. She is asleep within minutes so I ease from the bed to go clean myself up in the bathroom.

Only minutes later, I climb back into the bed with her pulling her close. That was the best feeling after an orgasm I have ever felt is my last thought before sleep claims me as well.

Miranda

The next morning I expect to be alone in the bed but I wake up to Blood's huge arms holding me close. I swear that was the best sleep I have had in ages.

I just lay still in his arms not wanting to wake him as I don't know how things will be between us since what we did in the night. Will he pretend nothing happened? Why did he not want to do more than use his hands?

"I can hear the wheels in that beautiful head turning." He whispers but causes me to jump as I didn't know he was awake.

"I didn't realize you were awake."

"Been awake for over an hour. Just didn't want to let you go just yet." He emphasizes by pulling me even closer.

"Did you sleep okay? I didn't hurt you or anything did I?" He asks gently.

"I slept better than I have in a long time. And no, you did not hurt me. It felt wonderful."

"Good. Now, we really should get up. I am sure breakfast has long since been ready and I am starving." He says as he gets out of the bed.

Several hours later, we are all outside building snowmen. Little Hanley is still convinced that Blood is a giant and has declared that he has to build a giant snowman that she can take a picture with.

He is so good with her causing me to wonder where he got so much experience with children. We haven't talked much about his family. I am not sure he even has any. There are no pictures in his room to indicate otherwise. So I decided to just ask him.

"Do you have any family?" as soon as it's out of my mouth he seems to go still as if afraid of the answer.

"Why are you asking?"

"You are so good with little Hanley, I just figured you have to have some family somewhere to get that kind of experience in dealing with them." I hurriedly explain.

"I have a little sister. Our parents were not worth a shit and it fell on my shoulders to take care of her from the time she was born."

"Oh I'm sorry. Guess it is a touchy subject and shouldn't have asked." I look down afraid that I will cry for him but he lifts my chin with his finger.

"I don't mind answering questions about myself for you Angel. My sister would really like you. I am actually surprised I haven't heard from her in a few days. Which worries me somewhat."

"Why does it worry you?" I ask curiously.

"She doesn't pick the best men to attach herself to. Far as I know the one she has been dating recently doesn't hurt her but he's not nice either. I have been trying to stay out of it as it is her life to live. I had been planning on a trip to see her, hopefully to run the fucker off but we got busy with what happened in New Orleans."

"So I have put a huge dent in your plans and in your life?"

"Not at all. You may not realize this yet but eventually you will. You are just as important to me as my sister is." He leans in kissing my forehead, his words are like a soothing salve I didn't know I needed.

Blood

"It's great to have you back man!" Snake says as he slaps Wrench on the back.

"It feels pretty good to be back. Being able to have a beer without thinking it might get shot out of my hand is a damn good fucking feeling!" Wrench throws back his beer and downs it then signaling for Fang to bring him another.

"I'm surprised Fang and Dane haven't been patched in yet." he comments looking at Timber.

"Just a formality at this point really. We need to do it sooner rather than later though. We also need to be looking for new prospects or the patched members will have to start doing all the shitty jobs again." Timber chuckles at the thought.

"Fuck that! We'll find some prospects as soon as it warms up again!" Bear grumbles from the other table.

"Hello Mister Giant!!" I hear squealed as tiny feet run my way from the hallway.

I catch her as she leaps into my lap.

"Hello Miss Hanley. How are you? You didn't get too cold making giant snowmen earlier did you?"

""No sir! But mommy said I just had to have a bath. I hate taking a bath! Why do I have to have one when I'll just get dirty again." She shrugs her shoulders as if truly perplexed by the idea and I can't help but smile at her.

"I am so sorry Blood. She gets gone fast." Hayden says as she walks into the room.

"She is fine. I enjoy talking with her."

"Well we are headed into the kitchen with the other girls for a snack. Come on Hanley; let the men have their quiet time." She says as she picks the little girl up and walks towards the kitchen.

"That your woman Blood?" Wrench asks while looking in the direction Hayden went.

"No. My woman's name is Miranda. That one was Hayden. She owns the workout studio in town that the women go to. Her car slid off the road from the ice causing her to be stranded here."

He grunts by way of an answer. That is one thing he and I have always had in common. If a grunt will do, that is our answer. No sense in wasting words.

We sit around catching up with Wrench for another hour plus filling him in on everything that has been going on.

Timber made some calls that will hopefully put us in touch with Antonino "Tony" Marcus. The head of the Marcus family in New Orleans.

Now all we can do is wait. I plan to use the time to make Miranda fall in love with me.

Chapter 7
Miranda

It took five days for the blizzard-like weather to stop. The snow plows have been clearing the roads. Everything is still frozen but at least we can go to town again as long as we are in the four wheel drives.

Blood has been so sweet to me the last few days. We've talked about all kinds of things. I also found out that his real name is Christopher Owens.

I've taken to calling him Chris when we are alone or when he is annoying me. It seems to really get his attention when I do so.

He's opened up more about his family. Well, he's been more open about his sister. Her name is Lacy and she lives a few towns over.

She's an amazingly talented tattoo artist that apparently picks men who like to use her for her money. I can understand why they can't see eye to eye on her boyfriends from the stories he has told me. I wouldn't like them either.

He has been looking at a building to buy in town that she could possibly use as a tattoo shop. It comes with an apartment above the shop that would be perfect for a single woman. Or so he says. I did volunteer to look at it with him to see what I think about it before he pitches the idea to Lacy. I like that he is interested in my opinion.

He hasn't touched me again sexually and I am beginning to feel self conscious about it. So I have decided to make the first move tonight. He's already in the bed waiting for me to get out of the shower. I decided to just towel off and walk into the bedroom completely naked before I lose my nerve.

I open the door, stepping into the room. The only light is coming from the T.V. but he sits straight up as soon as he sees me.

"Angel?" he growls as if he is having a hard time breathing.

I don't say a word as I walk over to the side of the bed he is now sitting up on. Grabbing his face, I bend down to kiss his lips.

"I need you Chris. Please?" I sigh into his mouth as his hands grab my hips.

Blood

Watching her walk out of that bathroom completely naked has my entire body going rock hard instantly. It takes everything I can muster to hold my desire back from grabbing her as she bends down to kiss me.

"Oh fuck! You are so beautiful!" I whisper to her as I pull her more fully on top of me.

I take my time rubbing her beautiful curves with my rough hands and watch as chill bumps are left in my path. Her nipples become hard points that are begging to be in my mouth.

"Are you sure you are ready for this Angel." I whisper to her barely controlling myself.

"God yes!" As soon as she answers I pull her forward until I can cover her core with my mouth, sucking deep and thrusting my tongue as far as it can go.

Her taste is sweet on my tongue. As I hold her to my mouth with one hand, I remove my shorts with the other. My too hard cock springing free to slap against my stomach. I have never wanted a woman as much as I want her.

I feel she is close to orgasm as her walls begin to squeeze my tongue so I thrust even deeper and harder until she screams out.

Before she has time to completely catch her breath, I pull her back down my body, her wet pussy leaving her sweet juice on my chest. Setting her core directly on my cock, I rub back and forth making sure to hit her clit each time with the tip making her moan.

Holding her up until I can line my cock up with her passage, I hold there looking deep into her eyes. Afraid to see fear in her eyes. Not seeing any doubts on her face, I slowly lower her until she is fully seated on top.

She feels so tight wrapped around me that I feel like I might pass the fuck out if I have to stop now. Without me moving another muscle, she lifts herself up and back down slowly as if testing herself.

It doesn't take her long to speed up her pace. I want so badly to slam her down onto me each time but I settle for pushing up just a little more as she comes down.

"Fuck Angel, I'm close. I need you to cum now." I growl, barely able to hold off my own orgasm.

She continues to ride me, moaning my name over and over. I know she is close again as her walls begin to tighten around me, choking my cock.

"Cum right fucking now Angel!" I demand as I slam upwards into her. As soon as my demand is out, her wet heat squeezes my cock once more in a death grip. Feeling my own orgasm starting to explode. I pull out of her and cum all over us both.

Miranda

Last night was absolutely amazing. Being on top I am sure is the reason I didn't have a freak out plus the fact he never held me tightly as if I couldn't get away if I wanted to.

Thinking about the way that he made me feel currently has me smiling like a crazy woman. The other girls have commented several times about a glowing look on my face. I know that they know exactly what my smile is from which causes me to smile even more.

"Oh, I meant to tell y'all! Timber talked to Hayden about coming here on certain days, starting today; to work with us in the facility we have on the grounds. She'll be here around noon today!" Mina says excitedly.

"Cool! So we don't actually have to go into town? I like that idea so much better. Especially with everything that went on last time!" I sigh with relief.

"You are getting better though. We have all noticed you are less jumpy these days." Bella says with encouragement.

"She's right. You didn't freak out yesterday when Wrench let the front door slam. Although it was still awesome to see Blood freak out for you." Mina laughs as we all smile at the memory of my giant man running into the room cussing whoever let the door slam.

"Poor Wrench didn't know what was going on." I chuckle. "Talking to the therapist has helped a lot."

"I haven't pushed you to talk about it but hopefully you know you can talk to both of us about what you went through." Mina looks at me with a look that clearly says that I am one of them.

"It's from being in a box you know? That's how they transported us down south. In boxes that were made like caskets. They had tiny breathing windows on the sides. Along the trip, the men would pick one of the boxes and that is who they'd do things too. The rest of us could only lay there and listen as she screamed. Most of the time, the other men would beat on all the other boxes egging each other on as they watched the show." I didn't realize that I had started to cry until both Mina and Bella wrapped me into a hug.

"Did they ever get you out?" Mina whispers softly as if afraid of my answer.

"No. I've felt so bad about that. That I escaped without going through that while some of the others didn't. I laid there in that box every time, praying they'd pick someone else. I'd feel so bad afterward for hoping so hard they'd pick one of the others instead of me."

"You can't do that to yourself. I've been there myself. I felt as though I should have died with my baby. It wasn't meant to be though. I am here. I have baby Justice, Blade and this little one on the way. I am still sad for my first baby but life does go on. It will get easier as time passes. I promise it will." Bella says as they both hug me tighter.

"I am so glad to have all of you in my life now. Thank you for being here." I say through the tears.

"Hey, I know what will make you feel better! Let's go ride the snow machines until Hayden gets here." Bella suggests with a huge smile.

"You really think Blade will be okay with you riding the snow machine?" Mina asks with skepticism.

"I don't exactly plan to announce it. You planning to rat me out?" Bella gives her a piercing stare until we all start to laugh.

"Hell no I ain't ratting you out! Let's go have some fun!" Mina says as she jumps up from the table.

Blood

Timber called for an emergency meeting after getting a phone call an hour ago. Most of the guys were already here at the clubhouse but we have been waiting for Blade to get back from whatever errand he was sent on with the prospects. As they all file into the room, Wrench shuts the door before Timber starts to speak.

"I received a phone call a little more than an hour ago from an associate of Tony Marcus. Apparently he has been out of the states for a little more than a year. He left his son in charge down in New Orleans. From what the associate says, Tony Marcus has no idea about what has been going on down in New Orleans."

"How is that even possible? Does he not keep up with what his own son has been doing with his so-called company? I totally call bullshit on this one." Bear commits from his side of the table.

"I have to agree here Prez. How does the head of the family not know what's been going on?" I ask with confusion.

"From what I found, his son has been able to silence everyone because they are afraid of him. Mr. Marcus took most of those that are completely loyal to him along on his trip to South America." Snake says from in front of his laptop he always has with him.

"In other words, while Daddy has been away, the son has been running loose to do whatever the hell he wants?" Butcher shakes his head, completely disgusted with it all.

"So what does this associate say about what they plan to do about it?" Blade asks Timber.

"The associate's name is Baratta. He should be here within the next few days ahead of his boss. Mr. Marcus wants Baratta to help us find Ray Stein. He wants him alive. I am assuming so he can get the proof he needs against his son down in New Orleans. Snake, until he gets here, I want you looking into who exactly this Baratta is. He didn't give a last name and I am fairly certain the phone number he called from was a burner."

"Sure thing Prez. I will start by accessing the FBI files on the Marcus family." Snake raises his eyebrows up and down at the thought of hacking them again.

"Just don't get caught." Timber chuckles as we all stand up to leave.

Miranda

"Oh my God this is so fun!!" Bella squeals as we come to a stop at the top of a ridge overlooking the clubhouse property below.

It is a huge piece of property at the base of a mountain. You can even see the cabins owned by the club aptly named, Wolfs Ridge.

"It's so beautiful up here." I sigh, mostly to myself.

"These views are what drew me to this area when I first came here. I remember thinking it would be the best place to write my books." Mina says as she walks up beside me.

"I think the two of you are nuts. But I have lived here my whole life so it's all I really know. I got to see quite a bit while I was away and I would have to say that my favorite view is the desert." Bella shakes her head decidedly.

"You are such a weird bitch." Mina smiles at Bella.

"You're the bitch!" Bella pokes her tongue out; all three of us begin to laugh.

"If we don't get back soon, there will probably be hell to pay with those men of ours." Mina finally says after a few minutes of us just taking in the scenery.

"You damn straight there will be!" We all jump at the sound of Fang's voice behind us.

"Damnit Fang! You scared the hell out of us!" Mina admonishes him while I marvel at the fact that I didn't have a complete melt down at being scared out of my wits.

"Karma will do that." Fang shrugs before grinning at Mina. "So I guess two of you can double up so that I can get a ride back."

"Why would we double up? Why can't you ride bitch?" Mina grins at him.

"Oh hell no! I will not ride bitch! And I most certainly will not ride up to the clubhouse with either of you three holding on behind me! I plan on living the rest of my life with all of my appendages still attached. Thank you very much." He says very seriously while Mina doubles over in laughter.

"You can have mine Fang; I'll ride double with Mina. That way you can keep all of your body parts. At least for today." Bella giggles as she climbs on behind Mina.

"Thank God! They are probably already waiting to kill me for letting you three slip away right under my nose as it is!"

"You can always claim we overpowered you." I say with as much innocence as I can muster.

"Like Hell!!" he growls, taking off on the machine, leaving our laughter in his wake.

Chapter 8
Blood

Snake dug as deep as possible trying to find anything on this Baratta guy. It is as if he's a ghost that really doesn't even exist. There were several mentions of him throughout the FBI files on the Marcus family but even they couldn't produce anything concrete on him.

The only picture they had labeled as possibly him was a really grainy black and white photo taken from behind which isn't helpful at all.

The FBI suspects him of having killed more than one hundred people without having left a single trace of himself behind at any of the scenes.

Knowing these details or lack thereof, we are fairly certain he is a man we do not want putting his cross-hairs directly on our club.

"Got a text from Baratta. He agreed to meet at the abandoned warehouse just outside of town. I thought it would be better than bringing him here around the girls. Snake, make sure the cameras you put out there are running correctly. I want a picture of this guy that we can run facial recognition on."

"They should be running perfectly. I keep a check on all systems we have installed periodically just in case we ever have a need. I will run a diagnostics to be absolutely sure so that we are not going in blind." Snake answers.

"Wrench, I need you to make sure that all the coms are in working order. The prospects will stay here with the women. We don't know this guy plus he works for the mob. Nothing good ever comes from being connected to them." Timber says to the room of men.

After going over the plans for tonight, we all file out to carry on the rest of our day as if nothing was going on.

I had just finished cleaning a carburetor for the sportster I was working on when Miranda walks into the shop.

"Looking for me Angel?" I smile as I wipe my hands on a shop rag.

"Yes I am. Are you about ready to eat? Dinner is almost ready and I know you like to get a shower before you eat."

Thoughts of possibly getting her naked and in the shower with me run through my mind. Sounds like a great plan to me.

Miranda

He has been grinning like a loon ever since I mentioned him getting a shower before we eat. As we walk into the bedroom, he turns around to shut the door. While staring at me begins to take his shirt off revealing that chiseled sexy chest of his.

"Your turn." His voice is huskier than before.

I know that he is now waiting for me to take my own shirt off so I do exactly that as I walk backwards towards our bathroom. Watching his eyes as I let my bra loose, my breasts springing forward, I see them change to a darker shade indicating his hunger for me.

When he finally makes it into the bathroom, all he sees is my back side as I step into the shower. Within a minute he is right behind me, his front touching my back as he wraps his arms around me.

He gets a hand full of my body wash and begins to wash me all over very slowly. It is the greatest pleasure my body has ever felt. His work roughened hands on my soft belly as he moves slowly down to the junction between my legs, causing a shiver to run down my spine.

His first touch to my clit has my body jolting forward as a sigh escapes my lips.

"You are so beautiful to me." he whispers as his thumb light strums on my clit for a few seconds then stopping as he turns me towards him as he goes down on his knees in front of me.

He leans forward sucking my clit into his mouth. All I can do is moan as my head goes back against the shower wall. My knees start getting weak, not wanting to hold my body up as a tingling sensation begins to build deep within. I am so close and about to explode when he quickly pulls away.

Standing up, he lifts me by my thighs with his arms, slowly sliding me back down onto his cock. We both sigh as he pulls me completely down onto him.

"God, woman, I love the way you feel all wrapped around me." He growls just before his mouth takes mine.

While still kissing me deep, he begins lifting me up very slowly until only the tip of his cock is still inside and then slamming me down onto him going as deep as possible.

"I need you to cum Angel, I won't last much longer. You feel too fucking good."

It only takes a few more times until I am exploding around him. He picks up his pace as soon as I cum, slamming into me hard and fast until I feel him start to explode. He doesn't pull out this time and I can feel the heat of his cum inside of me.

I am on the pill so that isn't too big of a problem. I do hope that one day; we might have a little one of our own. I love him; I have for quite a while. I only hope he loves me just as much as I already do him.

Blood

We get to the meeting spot a half hour early. Snake watched the feed on the surveillance cameras all afternoon to be sure no one came before we did to rig the place or to set us up. Far as he could see, no one has been here since the last time we used the place over a year ago.

Right at 9pm, headlights turn into the long drive coming to a stop just behind our own vehicles. We were unable to ride our bikes as there is still way too much snow on the ground. So we brought the cages we all ride in during the winter months.

A well dressed man in a suit steps out of the driver seat. He looks like a military man with the way his hair is cut and the way he carries himself.

"Good evening gentlemen." he murmurs in an accent that I can't quite place.

"I assume you are Baratta? I'm Timber and these are my club brothers, Blade, Wrench and Blood." Timber introduces us as we all look each other over like we are assessing an enemy.

"Mr. Marcus would like all of us to work together to find this Ray fellow. He would truly appreciate it if we could deliver him alive as he needs him to answer a few questions about Mr. Marcus' son's activities while he has been out of the states. Will this be satisfactory to you or will we have a problem?" Baratta asks Timber directly as if to intimidate our president.

"That is more than satisfactory as long as we can ensure the safety of Miranda Grayson." Timber answers with a steely voice.

"Ah, yes. The secretary. I assure you, Mr. Marcus has no designs at all against the poor woman. He is very upset that his son has caused so many problems where she is concerned. As well as all the other women." Baratta answers as if he is bored.

"I'm sure." I growl out loud causing him to turn his cold and lifeless looking eyes my way.

"Blood is it?" at the shake of the affirmative at his question, he continues. "While Mr. Marcus does not run business completely on the right side of the law, he is not into the selling and raping of women. He abhors such behavior."

"What does he plan to do to stop his son from continuing what he is doing?" Blade asks.

"That will be between Mr. Marcus and his adopted son. The only reason I am meeting with you is because Mr. Marcus requested that I do so. To show good faith. Otherwise I would have come into your territory, extracted Ray Stein and disappeared without any of you being the wiser." He speaks with so much confidence we are all sure he is speaking the truth. Not even the FBI has anything on this guy.

"I assume that you already have a plan?" Timber asks.

"Oh, I already have Ray Stein. I just need somewhere to store him and a place to sleep until Mr. Marcus gets here beginning of next week." He answers without a care in the world as he checks his watch as if late to get somewhere else.

"You already have him?" I ask, confused.

"Yes. He's in the trunk. Now, might I ask for a room to stay in while we await my boss' arrival?"

"We would have to ask that you not let on to any of the girls who you are exactly. Also that you behave yourself."

"You have my word as a gentleman." He smiles as he answers.

Driving back to the clubhouse I have to voice my opinion to Timber.

"I don't know about this Prez. Something tells me we are still in the dark. He isn't telling us everything."

"I agree with Blood. Something is up." Blade says from the front seat.

"Guess we'll just have to let it all play out. All of us need to be very vigilant in keeping an eye on all the women. Don't let any of them be alone. Keep a brother with them at all times." Timber says as we pullback up to the clubhouse.

Miranda

I am already in the bed, propped up watching the T.V. when Blood comes back from wherever it was the guys went earlier. He wouldn't tell me, just said it was club business. I have already been informed that club business means we women don't need to know.

"What are you watching Angel?" He asks as he bends down to kiss me on the head before pulling his clothes off to get in the bed next to me.

"It's a hallmark movie about a princess that is tired of being a princess. She just wants to be a normal person for a day so she switches places with another girl that looks like her."

"Let me guess, while in the other girls' shoes, she finds her prince and falls in love?" He gets under the covers and pulls me into his arms.

"Something like that." I giggle at how accurate he really is about the movie.

"I love to hear you laugh." he whispers while looking directly into my eyes.

"I know what I love." I whisper back holding his eyes with my own.

"I already know. You told me last night in your sleep." He pulls my mouth to his, kissing me lightly. "And I love you my beautiful Angel." he says against my lips before kissing me deeper.

We fall asleep wrapped around each other while trying to finish the movie. My last thought before sleep claimed me was that nothing could ever make me as happy as he did tonight with his admission of love. Everything I have ever looked for in a man comes in a package covered in tattoos and wearing a leather vest.

Life with this man will never be boring. He also brings with him even more family. The one thing I have always wanted ever since my family died. Yes I had my Uncle but I missed my parents and older brother more than anything in the world.

I hope Blood wants a lot of kids. While we already have a large family when counting the club members, I want several little ones of our own.

Falling asleep, I forgot all about letting Blood know that his sister called to say that she would be here tomorrow night and wanted to talk to him about something important.

Chapter 9
Blood

The next day we all take turns spending time where the girls are hanging out. Mina being the only one to take notice and seem super suspicious although she never voiced it out loud.

Growing up in the club life she already knows when to stay quiet. Baratta was introduced to the girls as a possible client for a custom build.

What was truly surprising was that he had a vast knowledge about bikes and admitted that he owns a custom softail bike that he enjoys riding when his schedule permits it.

Under any other circumstance, I could find him to be a guy I could easily get along with.

Since we still had jobs that needed done out in the shop, Timber invited him out there to watch as we work. It would also help to know where he is at all times easing our worries for our women. Especially since we all have the feeling he is not being completely honest in some way.

"Do you all get a lot of business for custom bikes way out here?" Baratta asks as he circles around the current bike I am working on.

"We get quite a few from all over the world. We don't maintain a website; most of our business comes in by word of mouth." Timber answers as he walks up next to him.

The phone starts to ring from the office so Timber excuses himself again to go answer it.

"Busy man." Baratta comments looking towards the office.

"It'll be spring soon which means the phone line will stay a lot busier as the days get warmer. More people will want to be on their bike than in a cage." I tighten a bolt before standing back up.

"A bike does make one feel more free." he murmurs just as Timber comes back.

"Damn that phone!"

"Mina already told your ass that you needed to hire someone to answer the phone, take messages and all that shit." I laugh at Timber's disgruntled look.

"I'll get around to it. I just don't think having a female in the shop all day would help some of our brothers get shit done!"

"One of your women couldn't do that for you?" As soon as Baratta asks the question, I know the perfect solution.

"That is a perfect idea. Miranda might be interested in the job. She'll want to go back to work soon." I look at Timber to gauge his reaction.

"Yeah, that would be perfect. I wouldn't have to worry about the single brothers wanting to fuck off all day chasing tail unless they wanted you to kill them." His eyes light up at the prospect as he thinks it over some more. "Hell yeah! Make sure and ask her. She can start as soon as she wants to. Let's go have a few beers!"

Miranda

Most of the Saturday nights that I have been here, I stay in our room after eating dinner not wanting to be in the crowds that begin to trickle in. Some weekends have gotten pretty wild, at least from what I can hear over the T.V.

However, tonight the girls have convinced me to hang out with them and so far I am having a lot of fun. It feels wonderful to laugh again. Surprisingly, even Uncle John is still here, laughing and joking with the guys.

"Hey Blood! Your sister is here!" Fang yells from the bar at the same time a beautiful dark haired woman with tattoos up both arms stops next to our table.

"I had to meet her over the fucking phone! Seriously Chris?" she crosses her arms over her chest as she glares at her brother.

"Watch it half pint! And when the fuck did you talk to Miranda on the phone?" Blood asks as he looks at me then at his sister again.

"It's nice to officially meet you." I say as I extend my hand in her direction. Instead of shaking my hand, she walks around to me and engulfs me into a hug.

"Hopefully you can teach the big oaf some manners. He desperately needs some!" She sticks her tongue out at him until he grabs her for a hug as well.

"What are you doing here anyway?" he asks now with concern.

"I was hoping Timber might have an open cabin at Wolf's Ridge."

"I think there's one that just opened up yesterday. The girls were planning to clean it first of the week before renting it out again. How long are you staying?"

"Indefinitely I hope. I packed up everything into a UHaul that is sitting out front. My lease was up on the building I was using for the shop and the owner was looking to sell the whole block to a developer." she shrugs at the end of her explanation.

"That sucks half pint but I think it will work out fairly well. The club may have the perfect spot for you in town if you are interested. We can go over the details with Timber tomorrow."

"Seriously? You have always been my favorite brother you know." She smiles wide at him.

"Hey. I'm your only brother." he growls.

"Psst. Minor details." She rolls her eyes at him.

"Half pint!" Timber's voice booms as he walks up with the man introduced to us as Baratta.

As Fiona turns in his direction, she goes eerily still as her eyes land on Baratta. I look at him just in time to see his eyes widen and his mouth lift in a tiny smirk. No one else seems to notice the tension between the two so I say nothing to Blood as Fiona finally relaxes and let's Timber pick her up into a bear hug.

"Why didn't you let us know you were coming? We've missed you." Timber says with all seriousness.

"I've missed all of you too. But hopefully you'll be seeing a whole lot more of me."

"Really? You finally leave that last asshat and decide to come back home?"

"Yes. I did." her look seems to change a little causing everyone at the table to look at her fully.

"Did he do something the rest of us need to know about half pint?" Blood growls.

"Nothing I couldn't handle. I promise. I don't want to talk about it. He's gone and that's that. Now, I am going to get a beer!" She spins on her high heeled boots and marches to the bar. Fang says something to her that causes her to throw her head back laughing.

"I assume she is family?" Baratta asks in his thick accent.

"Oh yeah, she's Blood's sister. She's a tattoo artist. Has actually made a name for herself. They just did a huge interview with her for a magazine. We are all very proud of her." Timber smiles in Fiona's direction.

Looking over at Blood I see that he is not smiling at all. In fact he is glaring at Baratta. Looks like he noticed something between them like I did.

Blood

The girls left this morning headed to town for more cleaning supplies to help Fiona get her cabin ready to move her stuff into it.

Since Miranda went with them, I figure it's the best time for me to make a visit to the back shed where Ray is being held. Timber made me promise to keep my temper in check and not kill the mother fucker since Marcus wants him alive for information to help him with his son.

As we walk into the shed, I can see Ray hanging from the ceiling by his wrists. Some of the guys must have taken his shoes and he currently smells like piss.

"I sprayed him down with soap and water but the mother fucker still stinks worse than horse shit!" Dane complains from the doorway while holding his nose.

"We haven't even done anything to your ass and you are already shitting yourself?" I ask as I get closer to him.

I watch as he raises his head, smiling in my direction.

"I'm not afraid of you bastards!" he spits in my direction almost getting his spittle on the toe of my boot.

"Maybe you aren't afraid of them. But you are afraid of me. No?" Baratta walks in, lighting up a cigarette.

Ray's eyes widen as he watches Baratta walk slowly closer.

"Ghost." Ray says barely above a whisper.

"Please! You have to tell Mr. Marcus that Joey did all of this. I will help him with everything. I swear it. Just don't kill me. Please!" he begs as he also begins to shake.

"If my orders were to kill you, I'd have done so the other night when I took you from your flea ridden motel room." Baratta murmurs with disgust. "As it stands, my boss would like to speak with you first. I really had rather just kill you. You've no idea what I think of a man that could do what you did to a woman."

"That fucking bitch should have died! I paid them bastards extra to torture her!" Ray's face is covered with rage. "She's the fucking reason I am in this mess!"

Before the last word is completely out of his mouth, my fists have already started swinging. I don't stop until I feel my brothers arms wrapped around me, pulling me away as they say my name.

Once they have me outside, they let me go as I scream out in my own rage.

"That mother fucker expected, even wanted her to die! I want to see his fucking blood draining from his body!"

"I will make certain you get that chance, once Mr. Marcus gets what he needs from him." Baratta stands in front of me with a sinister look on his face. "As long as I get to watch."

His words plus the fact I can tell from the look in his eyes that he is serious, is what finally calms me down. I shake my head in the affirmative as Dane hands me a beer.

Miranda

The girls and I finished up our shopping trip and decided to go eat lunch at Bella's Brew. Bella had called ahead to let her mom know we were coming by so that she could save a table for all of us. The lunch crowd is still out in full force so the place is packed.

"Mom saved us the table in the back. You all go sit down and I'll go get our food from the kitchen myself."

"Is she working any less now that she is pregnant plus having the little one?" Fiona asks.

"Blade tries to get her to cut back on her hours and he has succeeded a little bit. But, you know Bella." Mina shrugs.

"Yeah. Blade might as well chain her to the bed I guess if he doesn't want his child born on the floor in the back." Fiona's comment makes us all laugh at the thought.

Bella comes back to the table with one of her waitress's right behind her with our order.

"So, Fiona, how do you know this Baratta guy?" Mina looks directly at her while taking a bite of her burger. Bella and I sit quietly waiting to see if she denies knowing him which she does.

"I don't know what you mean. I've never seen him before." aching as nonchalant as possible but unable to look Mina in the eye.

"I can tell you are lying. Not yet sure as to why though. You know none of us will tell your secrets."

"You all won't say anything in front of any of the guys? You have to absolutely swear it!" She looks at each of us as we promise to keep whatever she says to ourselves.

"Okay." She sighs. "Bella, do you remember when I was invited to that Inkers Expo down in New Orleans?"

"Yeah, it was a bit more than a year ago. Wasn't it?"

"Yes. The night before I was to leave from there, I went with some of the other artists to a club just to hang out plus possible make a few more connections to get my name out there. Anyway, right when I was getting ready to leave was when I first saw him in the corner while I was on the balcony." She begins to smile as she remembers.

"Well I certainly don't want all the dirty details but who exactly is he?" Mina smiles.

"Speak for yourself on the details! We pregnant bitches need new ideas!" Bella wags her eyebrows up and down. We all laugh as Fiona throws a French fry at Bella.

"You are a fucking freak!" Fiona says to her. "Honestly? I have no idea who he is other than his name is Baratta. We didn't share much that night. At least not those kinds of details." Fiona shrugs.

"Do you all want to know my opinion on it all? Because honestly, things have been kind of odd lately if you haven't noticed." Mina looks at each of us seriously.

"I've noticed the prospects being on duty to watch the back shed. Actually I think it started the day Baratta showed up." Bella's eyes widen as Mina shakes her head.

"Exactly. They have someone in that back shed and I think it is Ray Stein." Mina whispers across the table and my own eyes widen at the thought.

"He's connected to the Mob. That could be who Baratta actually works for. You met him in New Orleans Fiona, which is where they are from!" I whisper back as I cover my face with my hands.

My heart starts to race but I start my breathing exercises like the therapist taught me to do. A minute later and I am fine again.

As I remove my hands, I see all the girls patiently waiting for me to become calm again.

I love these women for always knowing what I need.

"I'm good. Carry on." I announce as I take a sip of my coke.

"What do you think about getting a little pay back from that sick bastard?" Mina asks, dead serious.

"You girls would help me do that?" I whisper back.

"Hell yeah we would!" they all three say at once and then start laughing as if we aren't talking about something that could get us all put away for life.

"But how will we get past the guard?" I wonder out loud.

"Don't worry, I already have a plan." Mina begins to smile in a way that I have never seen before. *It's kind of scary but damn if I'm not totally in!*

Chapter 10
Blood

After going off the way I did on Ray, Timber called in our doctor friend that keeps our activities to himself so that he could check him over. We would definitely hate for Tony Marcus to get here and the fucker is already dead.

He didn't seem to have any major injuries other than bruises. Too bad. If they had left me alone, he'd either be dead or sporting some serious scars.

"Doc leave?" I ask Timber as he takes a seat next to me at the bar.

"Yeah, he gave him a sedative to knock him out so that Fang could get the stinky fucker cleaned up." He shivers, remembering the smell.

"I had to clean my arms up after too. It's all I could smell even while covered in his blood. Where's Baratta?" I ask as I look around for him.

"He's on the phone outside with his boss."

"You think we can trust this Tony Marcus? I mean we are talking about the Mob here."

"I'm not really sure yet. Guess we will find out what he's made of tomorrow when he gets here. Baratta doesn't seem so bad although Snake still hasn't found anything about him. I mean nothing. Not even a driver's license."

"Did you hear the name Ray called him?" I ask quietly.

"I texted Snake right after we pulled you off of Ray. He's cross referencing the nickname in every database he can access as we speak."

"Good. There's something about him that just doesn't sit right with me."

"That wouldn't have more to do with the look I saw you give him last night when he asked about Fiona would it?" Timber looks directly at me.

"He has no fucking business looking at my sister like that!" I growl into my beer.

"Your sister is a looker, always has been. You can't completely blame him for looking. You also need to get used to men looking at her like that. She's not a child any longer, she can take care of herself and you don't want her to move away again because of you messing in her relationships."

I curl my lip up at the thought of her dating but do realize Timber has a point. Ever since she moved away from White Summer, I have felt like it was my fault for her leaving.

We had a huge fight about the type of guys she was dating at the time. A few weeks later she came up with the idea to move away. I don't want that to happen again.

Miranda

Getting back to the clubhouse, Bella, Fiona and I head inside as Mina goes on a mission to get our supplies. She said she knew the perfect thing to use for my revenge. And knew exactly where to find it.

I shiver just at the thought but smile as well. Too bad for Ray that I know what he truly fears and it's something that most little boys absolutely love to play with. Where Mina could find such things during winter in Montana is beyond me but I didn't ask for details.

Seeing Blood sitting at the bar, I head in his direction, taking a seat next to him.

"Hey Angel. Have fun shopping with the girls?"

"Yep. We even went by Bella's Brew to eat lunch."

"Any problems?" He looks fully at me and I know what he is asking.

"Not really. Almost had one panic attack but I did the breathing exercises I've been learning. Calmed myself without a problem. It was great!" I smile wide.

Hearing someone call my name, I turn in that direction to see my Uncle John coming through the door.

"Uncle John! What are you doing here?" I stand up to hug his neck.

"Just thought I would swing by and let you know that all the new doors were installed today. The new windows should be done later this week, as well as the new alarm system on the house. SO you should be able to move back home soon." He smiles at me as I lose a little bit of my excitement from earlier.

"Oh, well, that's great I guess but I am planning on selling it. I just can't imagine staying there after everything that happened." I murmur as I look over at Blood who clearly is not smiling.

"I figured that would make you happy. To be able to go back home. But I guess I can't blame you for not wanting to go back." My Uncle says with understanding.

He stays for only a few more minutes before having to leave for work since he is on night shift. It takes Blood only a few minutes after he leaves to ask me about my plans.

"So you want to sell your house?"

"Yes but I will need to find another place soon. I mean, I love being here with you. Plus the girls mean the world to me. But we can't live in that tiny room forever, Blood." I explain, hoping that he will understand.

"WE can't?" he smiles realizing that I said we and not just I.

"No. WE can't." I smile as he pulls me into his lap and covers his mouth with mine.

"We can get the next cabin that becomes available at Wolf's Ridge." He suggests a few moments later.

"Those cabins are definitely beautiful. Do you think there will be an availability soon?" My mind starts going over the possibilities of living in one of the cabins.

"We'll check with Mina about it." He says as he kisses my forehead with a smile.

Blood

Once all the women head off to bed, we all sit around just shooting the shit.

"So why not tell us why Marcus doesn't know what his son has been up to while he's been out of the country." Snake asks from his seat.

"Well, it's not that he didn't exactly know, it's just he was more invested in what he went searching for in South America." Baratta answers as he relaxes farther into his seat.

"What was he searching for that was more important than his son selling and torturing women?" I growl down the table.

"The love of his life." Baratta murmurs quietly as the rest of us are not totally sure what to say to that.

"Did he find her?" Timber asks.

"Yes. But it's all very complicated. You see, Joey, is not actually his son. He is his brothers' son that he adopted after he died. He suspects Joey of being the one that caused Morgania's disappearance."

"Oh shit, that's fucked up. Why would he want to get rid of her?"

"She has a daughter named Markayla. Beautiful young woman. It has always been suspected that she is Mr. Marcus' true heir although he has never admitted as such." He shrugs. "Joey has also been unnaturally obsessed with her since she turned fourteen. When Morgania started to notice and voice her concerns, she went missing."

"If it is true, what will he do with his nephew?" Snake asks even though we all are curious as to the answer as well.

"What would you do?" Baratta asks looking at each of us.

"Nephew or not, he'd be six feet under." Bear, who is normally very quiet, speaks up from his chair at the bar.

"I'd have to agree with Bear." Timber says into his beer as we all shake our head in agreement.

Miranda

It only takes us an hour of waiting on Fiona to have everything we need. Carrying her load in a plastic bucket, Fiona puts them into the back of the SUV before we all pile in.

"One day you are going to have to tell us who your contacts are that can help get such things in the dead of winter." Mina says in all seriousness to Fiona as croaking sounds come from the back.

"Are you sure this will work?" Bella holds up the container of coffee Mina laced with sleeping pills.

"Absolutely! It's the same recipe I used to knock my brother Reaper out when I wanted to sneak out back in high school." She smiles at the memory.

"I'm not going to pull all the way up to the shed so Fang won't see you guys in the truck. Give me twenty minutes and then pull the rest of the way up." She says as she takes the coffee and gets out of the truck, walking towards the shed.

Twenty minutes later, we pull up and see Fang dead asleep on the ground.

"Holy fuck! You didn't kill him did you?" Fiona demands as she walks over to check his pulse.

"No! I'm a professional and know what I am doing!" Mina huffs as we begin to laugh.

"Come on; let's get this show on the road." Mina motions for us to follow her to the back of the SUV.

Watching as she opens the back, we immediately spot the box. A box that eerily looks similar to the one I was held in when they transported us down south.

"Where the ever loving fuck did you find this?" Fiona demands before I can say anything.

"In the old storage shed." She shrugs as if it were natural to have such a thing in storage.

We pull it out and open the top. There on the inside of the lid is what is clearly claw marks as if something or someone was desperately trying to get out. I should know as the one I was held in had the same thing by the time I was taken out of it. I shiver from the memories.

"You okay there, Miranda?" Mina asks softly.

"Yeah, I'm good." I shakily reply, still staring at the box.

"I'm not sure if I should now be afraid of the men I have known my whole life or be thoroughly impressed." Fiona who is also still staring at the box with wide eyes whispers causing everyone to laugh breaking the serious moment.

As we carry the box to the door, we hear something behind us. Turning in that direction, Baratta steps into the light. We drop the box in front of the door and freeze in place.

"Seems you have used all of whatever you gave that poor fellow. So how exactly do you women plan to get Mr. Stein into that box? I assume that is your plan?"

"Well Mr. Cocky, since you are here, YOU can help get him into the box." Mina crosses her arms waiting for him to refuse.

Surprisingly, he just smiles and walks the rest of the way to us, opening the door.

"Then grab your box and follow me."

"Seriously? You aren't going to rat us out?" I ask, stunned by his actions.

"You are not my women therefore I do not have a dog in this race. But, I will help to get him in the box so that none of you get hurt."

Walking in, the stench is overwhelming. It takes Ray a few minutes to look up to see who walked in. His lip curls up in disgust as he begins calling me all kinds of names.

"Shut up!" Mina screams and he turns in her direction. "Glad I can get your attention. A little birdy told me you are afraid of frogs. Is that true?" She waits a beat but he says nothing. "Guess we are about to find out. Baratta put him in the box please."

Within a few moments, he is locked up in the box as we all take turns dropping frogs into the hole on top. With each frog, his screams get louder and my smile gets wider.

Blood

A little after midnight we all get up to head to our rooms for the night. I catch Timber looking at his phone curiously.

"Something wrong Prez?" I ask and all the brothers stop to hear the answer.

"Fang hasn't checked in. I sent him a text twenty minutes ago and he still hasn't answered back."

"We should all go check it out. Let's check on the girls first though." Timber agrees and we all head to our rooms to check the girls.

It doesn't take long for us to realize that they are all missing.

"Oh fuck! Baratta isn't in his room either!" Snake slams the door to the room we gave to Baratta to use while he is here.

"Everyone grab your weapons. Meet outside in five minutes. Hopefully we find them quickly." Timber growls with worry.

I know what he is feeling. It took too long last time to find Miranda. We got lucky she wasn't more damaged by the time we got her out of that warehouse. It could have been worse.

"Hey! I checked the security feed. They are at the back shed! The one with Ray Stein and it looks like Fang is on the ground!" Snake hurriedly tells us as we move to the door.

It only takes a minute to pull up to the shed. Getting out, we quietly make our way over to Fang and check his pulse. He seems to just be asleep and unhurt but we are unable to wake him up. Just before we open the door, we hear all the women laughing like crazy.

Opening the door, we see the girls all passing around a bottle of liquor although Bella just passes the bottle on. Baratta is leaned up against the back wall shaking his head and Ray Stein is nowhere to be seen. All we can see is a box shaped like a coffin sitting in the middle of the floor.

"What the fuck is going on here?" Yells Timber which makes the girls all jump but Baratta just stays in the same spot he was in. "Where the fuck is Ray?" His question just pushes the girls into loud giggles once again.

"Care to fill us in on what the fuck you and the girls are doing here? And why is Fang knocked out cold?" I wait for Baratta to answer.

Pushing himself off the wall, he takes out a cigarette, lighting it up.

"They needed help getting him into the box. That I helped with. As for your prospect, the main lady there did that." He points to Mina.

"Ray is in there?" Points Snake. "Why?"

"That my friend you would have to ask your women. If they are not too drunk to answer you." He chuckles as he heads towards the door.

Right at that moment, we hear a chorus of frogs coming from the box.

"What the fuck is in there with him?" Dane demands sending the girls into peals of laughter.

Chapter 11
Blood

The next morning all the girls except for Bella, have a major headache as we sit down for breakfast.

The brothers talked it over last night before going to bed that we would not be easy on them this morning. So we all are making as much noise as possible.

"Okay. Now that all of you ladies are awake it's time to discuss your actions of last night. Whose hair brained idea was it to begin with?" Timber asks from the head of the table.

He looks over at Mina as if he knows that it was her. Hell, we all believe it was her. She grew up in this life so she would know how to plan it all out.

"Really? Not a single one of you are going to tell who thought it would be a good idea?"

"It was mine! I wanted to make him suffer after everything I went through. I talked all the girls into it. I'm sorry." Miranda speaks up on everyone's behalf.

"While I commend you for taking the blame, I find it highly unlikely it was you sweetheart. But that being said, I do believe that every one of you needs to be punished for what you did. I was very specific when I said where you ladies were and were not allowed to go. Was I not?" He looks at them all one by one until they each shake their head. "I think I will leave that up to your men to take care of. And I do not want to ever have to have this conversation with you all again. Are we clear?" He waits for them all to answer yes before he sits back down to finish his breakfast.

My sister being the smartass that she is raises her hand until Timber notices her.

"I don't have a man to take care of it." She smirks in his direction.

At that moment, I swear I heard Baratta murmur real low, "That could be remedied." But there was no way for me to be absolutely sure. So I just look in his direction but he continues to look at his plate as he finishes his eggs.

"I will think of a fitting punishment for you half pint, don't you worry about that! And furthermore, I think all of you owe Fang a huge apology for what you did to him!"

The women sit quietly as if truly chastised although we all know them better than that.

"One last question. Just where in the actual fuck did you all find frogs this time of year?" The girls all cut their eyes towards Fiona who pretends to have not heard the question. "You know what?" Timber sighs as he continues. "I don't even want to know." He shakes his head as everyone continues breakfast.

Miranda

I watch as Blood moves around the bedroom finding everything he needs. The guys have a meeting soon that will happen in the office at the shop.

"You girls are to stay inside this clubhouse until we get back. Understand?"

"Yes, we'll stay put. What did Timber mean by you guys giving us our punishment?" I ask out of curiosity.

"He means we should give you a spanking." He smiles in my direction.

"That doesn't sound too bad to me." I smile back at him through the mirror on the wall, surprising him.

Walking up behind me, he presses his front to my back and I arch into him. Thoughts swirl in my head at the possibilities.

"Are you getting wet thinking about my hand spanking that ass as I plow into you from behind?" He whispers into my ear.

"Yes." I groan as his cock hardens in his pants and presses into my ass.

"Uhmmm, too bad it has to wait for now. But just so you know, I will make sure you still feel the sting of my hand the next morning." He whispers as he nibbles on my ear before pushing away and heading out the door leaving me a whimpering turned on mess.

Getting back into the main part of the clubhouse, I find the other girls in the sitting area trying to find something to watch on the big screen. Fang is in a chair across the room still fuming.

"Fang, we really are sorry." I say to him.

"I may be the youngest in the club, but I am tired of you women treating me like I am just a kid! Mina, you embarrassed me in front of the other brothers." He throws the last part in her direction.

"I really am sorry Fang. I didn't mean to embarrass you. You know, even if it had been my Ol' Man on duty, I'd have done the exact same thing to him as well." She shrugs.

"Really? You'd have done that to Timber?" He asks with skepticism.

"Absolutely. I did the same recipe on my brother Reaper when I was still in high school."

"What did he do?"

"He whipped my ass good is what he did. However, it did not stop me from doing it again or him falling for it again." Her admission gets everyone laughing.

"Just so you know I will NOT be falling for it again!" Fang declares as our laughter gets even louder.

Blood

Baratta left to go meet Tony Marcus at the airport before bringing him to the shop to speak with us. We left the women at the clubhouse with Fang and Dane watching over them. Hopefully they stay out of trouble until this meeting is over.

"Hey, I found a few mentions of "Ghost" in association with the Marcus family buried deep within the FBI case files." Snake sits his computer down on the table, clicks around a bit and moves back for Timber to look at it.

"What exactly am I looking at?" Timber asks as he looks over the page.

"Italian military records for a man named Alessandro Baratta, AKA Ghost. He is highly trained in warfare, hand to hand combat and was one of the greatest snipers in Italian history. He even received a highly decorated honorable discharge."

"That would explain how it's hard to find information on him with the military and government keeping it all hush hush. But how the fuck did he get mixed up in the Italian mob?" I ask with confusion.

"That part is what is interesting. Alessandro Baratta does not technically exist. Other than the records you see, there is no other paper trail. Not even a birth record. There is one mention of "Ghost" by an informant to the FBI. That informant has since gone missing." Snake answers with a shake of his head.

"What exactly was the FBI investigating at the time?" Timber asks.

"I have no idea. That part of the case files was completely gone. Only someone really high up could have erased files completely from the server like that."

Each of us were having deep thoughts about everything Snake was able to find when we hear vehicles pulling up. Snake shuts off his laptop and closes it up.

We watch as Baratta opens the back door of a car with tinted windows and a very well dressed man steps out.

His hair is gray at the temples but he doesn't look to be more than fifty years old. He turns holding his hand out, helping a beautiful woman out of the car.

"Good evening gentlemen." His accent is even heavier than Baratta's. "I am Tony Marcus and this is my wife, Morgania." He introduces himself with a smile.

"Nice to meet you. I'm Timber and these are my brothers."

"May we sit down somewhere gentlemen?" Marcus suggests.

"Of course." Timber looks over at Marcus' wife.

"I have no secrets from her so we can speak freely." Marcus smiles at his wife who takes a seat at a table we had set up earlier.

"The package you wanted still breathing is in a shed on the back part of the property here."

"Oh I had no doubt about that. Baratta has kept me well informed the last few days." He takes a seat next to his wife. "I understand that you have questions concerning a Miss

Grayson that was somehow involved with Raymond Stein."

"Yes. She belongs to Blood here and if need be we all will fight to the death to protect her." Timber looks him directly in the eye.

"That will not be an issue." Marcus waves his hand as if to dismiss the idea. "I do not condone such behavior as sex trafficking or the torturing of women. It is our job as men to protect them." He reaches over and holds his wife's hand. "You look as though you are unsure to believe me."

"Well we did look into your family. You are not exactly law abiding citizens." Snake says from his chair.

"Ah. But neither are any of you. I know all about every one of you, this club and even your women. You really didn't think I wouldn't have you all checked out too right?"

"Fair enough. So what now?" Timber relaxes a bit in his seat.

"We would like to find somewhere to stay a few nights before we head back to New Orleans to deal with my nephew. We'll take Ray back with us. Baratta will arrange that." He looks to Baratta who nods once.

"We have a cabin currently available if you are interested." Timber offers.

"What do you think sweet?" Marcus asks his wife who still hasn't said anything.

"That would be amazing. You know how much I love the mountains." She replies with a huge smile on her face.

"I'll get one of my men to show you where the cabin is so that you may get settled.

You both are also more than welcome at the clubhouse for dinner if you would like."

"I would like that very much! I was so hoping to meet the women Baratta was telling me about." Her face lights up as she looks toward Timber who looks over at Baratta.

"She knows about the box and the frogs." Baratta shrugs.

"Now don't you be getting any crazy ideas from these young ladies now sweet. My old heart can't take it." Marcus holds his hand to his heart while giving her a serious look.

"There is nothing wrong with your heart old man." She laughs as she walks toward their car.

"Not any more there's not." I overhear Marcus whisper as he watches his wife.

Miranda

I'm just getting out of the shower when Blood comes into the bedroom for the night. Dinner lasted longer than normal with having all the new company for the night.

I was completely blown away by how much I truly enjoyed spending time with Mrs. Marcus.

The Marcus family kept apologizing for what I went through, they even offered to 'fix' everything. I bet I could have asked for anything in the world and they would have made it happen, but everything I want is right here.

There is a gleam in Blood's eyes tonight, he is planning something. I'm willing to bet that something has to do with me. He has been giving me predatory winks all night. I might be in serious trouble here. The minute he locks the door behind him I know.

I slowly start to back away but suddenly Blood is right in front of me. He scoops me up into his arms and whispers in my ear, "I still owe you a spanking my Angel."

Before I can even blink my towel is gone and I am draped over his knees. I look up in confusion, wondering how we got from there to here so fast. However; I don't even have a minute to think when I feel the first smack of his hand on my ass. It takes a few seconds for the sting of pain to reach my brain.

Blood is mumbling something and I have to really pay attention for his words to make sense.

"Silly woman did you think I would let you put yourself in danger?" *Smack* his hand lands on a different spot. "I wonder how many of these it will take to teach you a lesson?" *Smack* "Did you think nobody would find out?" *smack.* Then he rubs my ass, as if trying to push the lesson in.

His hands wander over my cheeks and down into my folds. When he quickly pulls his hand back at what he finds. Yep, I am dripping wet and it's not from my shower. Blood looks at his hands for a second and if I didn't already know I was in trouble I knew now.

"So," He asks me," You like that huh? This isn't supposed to be fun; it's a punishment not playtime."

Then he begins to spank me more seriously. After about twenty I can feel the sting on my ass so badly that I want to cry but even worse my pussy is dripping wet, begging for him to fill me up.

Blood pulls me up so I am sitting on his lap now and wraps his arms around me. "When I came upstairs and you weren't in our room waiting where I expected you, I thought you had been taken again right under my nose. Angel you are my light, my heart and my life. Do you have any idea how that felt to think I lost you?"

OH MY GOD! I think there are tears in his voice. The spanking didn't bother me, it only turned me on but I made this big strong biker man cry. I feel my heart break at the thought.

I wrap my arms around him and promise I will involve him in any future mischief. Even though I am unsure if I can always keep that promise. I have a feeling that being friends with the girls will get me quite a few spankings over the years. The side of my mouth slightly lifts at the thought.

Blood slowly starts peppering my face with kisses as he maneuvers my body down onto the bed. I expect to get a fast hard fuck but instead he slows down. It's as if he wants to get to know my body all over again.

His hands cup my breasts but his lips haven't stopped kissing me. I can feel him lowering himself inch by inch. While he is focusing on me, he doesn't notice my hands creeping towards his glorious dick. I hear him suck in a breath as my fingers curl around his cock.

This! This moment when we are holding each other in the dark, when we are sharing our bodies and our souls connect makes the hell of the last few months disappear.

I stroke him as his mouth continues to leave a trail of kisses down towards my pussy. It's getting harder to hold on to his cock in this position but I don't want to let go. I might belong to Blood but he belongs to me.

Suddenly he is gone from my hand but something much better is happening. "Oh My God!" I scream as Blood's tongue starts lapping at juices flowing between my legs.

I look down watching his head move as he starts licking my pussy like it's his favorite food. I don't know how long I can hold on; he is taking his time making sure he doesn't leave a centimeter of pussy untouched. "Blood, Blood, Blood" I am chanting.

"Let go." he tells me. Like I even have a choice anymore. I scream as the most intense orgasm of my life rips through my body. Then he is up and over me but he is not moving. Just holding a plank position over top of my body.

"I love watching you come for me, My Angel." He says and slips into me. The moment his cock is buried inside me I lose all thought and ability to speak. I can only moan and grunt as he moves his dick in and out hitting every sensitive spot I possess.

I am close, so close. Suddenly Blood stops and pulls away. I whimper and reach for him, I want to pull him back into me, but he evades my reaching arms and flips me over.

"Get on your knees, Angel."

I draw my knees up under me and he slips into me from behind. This new angle fills me up even more. I don't think I can hold out much longer. Blood's hands are twisting in my hair; he pulls my head back as he thrust in and out of me. I can only scream as tremors ripple through me. Then I am lost in the darkness that overtakes my vision.

Just seconds after I experience a mind blowing orgasm I feel Blood follow me over the cliff. Breathless and exhausted he wraps his arms around me and together we fall into peaceful dreams. I am his and he is mine.

Blood

I wake up wrapped around my woman. Last night didn't exactly go as planned. I revealed more of myself than I intended to but Dear Lord the beautiful way her ass turned pink under my hands and the way her pussy dripped and begged for me. I couldn't help myself.

Miranda Grayson is my Angel, my everything. I look at her and feel like I am home. Not a location, not the club I have dedicated my life to. Angel is my home; I will do whatever it takes to keep her safe and by my side for the rest of our lives.

It is still early and after last night I don't want to disturb her sleep. We went a few rounds and I wore her out. So I snuggle as close as I can and with a smile on my face drift back to sleep.

I wake up again with a moan on my lips as I look down at my Angel sucking my cock. I could get used to waking up this way. I wrap my hands in her hair. She looks up at me with the most beautiful eyes and a smile on her face.

"Angel, Baby please don't stop." I beg.

She gets a twinkle in her eyes as she moves her mouth up and down, stroking my cock with her lips. She stops. As I'm about to beg for more, her tongue pokes out of her puffy lips and my Angel licks me like an ice cream cone.

Oh God, did I say Angel? This woman is no Angel; she is the devil in disguise, a temptress, a succubus. She sucks my cock back into her mouth and I can do nothing but thrust deep into her throat. She gags a little but when I try to pull back she pinches my thigh.

I can't take it anymore. I am going to blow but I don't want to cum in her mouth. I grab her by her shoulders and pull her off my cock. She whimpers as I do so. Dear God my woman is whimpering for my cock but I can't give in. I toss her on the bed and bury myself deep inside her core. I can't hold out long but I am right where I want to be as we orgasm together.

Miranda

Blood and I showered together this morning. Shower sex is not as fun they make it sound in books, but I am still ok with that.

I go to the kitchen to help the girls with breakfast. Usually the Yotes are in charge of cooking but we still have Mr. and Mrs. Marcus here, so the girls and I decided we wanted to prepare their food instead of subjecting them to the half dressed, sometimes crude, women of the club.

Mrs. Marcus is quickly becoming one of us, so I am not really surprised to find her in the kitchen with Mina, Bella and Fiona. As soon as I walk in the door she throws her arms around me. I'm a little surprised but this woman could easily be one of us.

"Come, I want to talk to you girls before the men come charging in." She says. Once she has our attention... She pulls cards out of her pocket and slips one to each of us. "This is my number; I want you each to have it. If you ever need me for anything and I mean anything. You call me. Promise me you will do so. I don't care if you just want to talk, if you need a break from all this testosterone or if you need a hitman. You call me!"

We laugh a little at her hitman comment although we all are fairly certain that she is dead serious about it. After hugs all around we get back to preparing breakfast.

Sitting down at the table with our men, I notice that Bella and Mina seem to sit a bit lightly and I can't help the giggle that escapes. I know what all of us were doing last night.

Blood puts his arm around me, while talking to Timber and I realize he didn't even know he did it. It was a reflex every time I am close to him he touches me in some way as if to reassure himself that I am there. I snuggle closer with a smile as I think about last night and how well he loved me.

I am right where I want to be. With Blood's arms around me surrounded by the people I have grown to respect and love. This is my family.

Chapter 12
Miranda

"God, I love the view from this porch!" Staring out over the landscape, I can see the mountain peaks in the distance still covered in snow while the flowers bloom around the flower beds.

"It is very beautiful." Looking over I see Blood looking right at me instead of the view in front of us.

You aren't even looking at the mountains!" I accuse with a smile.

"There's no need when I can look at your beauty."

"You are such a dork sometimes!" I throw a cushion from the swing at him as he laughs.

"Do you need another spanking?" His eyes lit up with his own question.

"You mean like the one I got because of the frogs?" I ask innocently. "Because if my memory serves correctly, that spanking worked more for my own favor than for yours."

"I wouldn't be too sure about that. You still couldn't sit without feeling the sting the next morning. All of you girls looked a bit uncomfortable that morning as a matter of fact."

"I had much rather had that spanking than the deal poor Fiona got."

"It wasn't that bad!" He protests.

"It is for someone who doesn't like to eat meat! I just know she gagged the entire time working with the local butcher."

"Mr. Johnson said she did and he was afraid she would throw up on the roasts so he put her to cleaning up instead. At the last cookout, she stayed as far away from the grill as she could get and she still gagged a little." He laughs out loud as I throw my last cushion at his head.

"I noticed Mina doing some gagging of her own. Guess that morning sickness is still hitting her hard."

"Not just the morning sickness. Her hormones have been insane. I heard her threaten to saw Timber up into tiny pieces and feed him to Mr. Johnson's pigs the other day just because he told her that her ankles look swollen. Then she turned right around and told Bella she hated her for looking so amazing while pregnant." I laugh at the memory.

"Hopefully you don't try to kill me when our time rolls around."

"I make no promises there big guy." I declare as I head into the cabin to check our dinner on the stove.

Blood

"We'll need everyone to pitch in with getting all of Fiona's new equipment moved into the building this week. The grand opening of Poison Pen is next Friday. She has a lot of big name clients coming as well as several magazines covering the event." Timber says from the head of the table.

"All of our customs should be finished or picked up by the owners this week. We purposely didn't schedule anything to come in until after the opening so that gets our full attention." Blade comments.

"As for security, it'll mostly be all of us. I do think a few of the big names are bringing in their own security detail but our focus is Fiona. Her name is getting out there so it's not far fetched that she may get creepers along the way." Snake adds to the conversation.

At that exact moment all of our phones start blowing up with rings and texts. Looking at each other in confusion, we reach for our phones.

"Bella is in labor!" Blade yells as he knocks over his chair in his rush to leave the room.

"Well, I guess that wraps up this meeting." Timber chuckles as we all watch Blade run around like his ass is on fire.

"If you'll grab his ass Prez, I'll go grab the girls so we can all get to the hospital." I comment as we all start laughing as we see Blade grab his hair as if he can't remember what to do.

Several hours later we are all crowded around the observation window looking into the hospital nursery as a nurse pushes a tiny bed over for us to see inside.

"Oh my God, she's so beautiful!" Miranda whispers from beside me.

"Yes she is." I whisper back.

"Yall see my gorgeous daughter?" Blade asks as he walks up the hall. "I can't believe she's here." He sighs as he looks at her. "She'll be in the room with Bella in a little bit and all of you can come in to see her."

His smile is so wide it's hard to connect this Blade with the one I have always known. The one that wouldn't think twice about gutting a man with one of his precious knives he loves so much.

"So what did you two decide for a name?" Timber asks.

"Victory. We named her Victory." Blade sighs in awe as he looks at his daughter.

"That is a perfect name." Miranda whispers as all the girls get tears in their eyes. They all know how much this little girl means to Bella after the things she suffered to get here. How much she means to us all.

Looking over at the way Miranda's face has lit up just looking at the baby, I wonder how beautiful she will look holding our own daughter or son.

"I love you so very much my Angel." I whisper into her ear. She looks up at my face, smiling wide.

"I love you but now you want one don't you?" She raises her brow at me.

"One of what?" I ask innocently.

"Don't act all innocent with me mister." She chuckles at me. "I've already asked the doctor about stopping the birth control pills." She admits with a small smile.

"After we see the baby for a few minutes, we are going home. It's time for a spanking." I whisper huskily.

"Sounds good to me." She whispers back as she pushes into my cock. *Damn I love this woman!* I think to myself.

Life will never be boring with her.

Sneak Peak
Poison Pen
Baratta's Darness

Baratta

The club is packed as I make my way to the balcony hoping to get some air. Finding a quiet spot on the far side, I sit and drink my scotch slowly while the boss finishes up his meeting inside. A few minutes goes by when a young woman walks out, stopping to look over the balcony to the street below. New Orleans is always a party town, especially on Saturday night.

She doesn't seem to notice me in the corner, but I happen to be good at blending into the shadows. My eyes are drawn to her, not just by her beauty but by the gorgeous tattoo that goes up one leg disappearing under her short skirt.

"Hey, we all are going to another local spot. Want to come with us?" I hear as another woman walks up next to her.

"Nah, I think I'll call it a night soon and go back to the hotel. My flight leaves pretty early." She responds in a sultry husky voice that immediately has me wondering what she would sound like with her legs wrapped around my head.

She stays in the exact same spot for several more minutes after the other girl leaves. As she turns around, she finally notices me as she jumps a little bit and her hand goes to her chest.

"I'm sorry. I didn't see you there." She smiles in my direction.

"I wasn't really trying to be seen." I respond as I take another sip of my scotch.

"Well, sorry." She says as she turns to leave.

"Where are you running off to?" I ask not really wanting her to leave which is completely out of character for me.

"Back to my hotel. I have an early flight." She smiles again and I catch my breath at her beauty yet again.

What the fuck is wrong with me? I think to myself. I am never impulsive. I calculate everything.

"So you are not from around here then?" I grin back at her as I lean forward, more into the light. I watch as her smile becomes even bigger.

Maybe I won't have to go very far for a fuck tonight after all.

Fiona

Today was a huge success for my business. Accepting the invitation to the Inkers Expo they were holding this year in New Orleans was the best decision I could have made. There were so many big names in the business here that would be able to get my name out there. There were several reporters that stopped to take pictures and ask questions about my work.

My dreams were coming true and I had my brother to thank for that. He and his club, The Wolfsbane Ridge MC, gave me my first loan to open up shop after they realized how much I loved to draw and eventually do tattoos. I don't use stencils to do my work, everything is by hand.

Finished with cleanup at my station, I begin packing all of my supplies back into my duffle bags when a couple of the girls I met here walk up asking if I want to go to the after party with them. I think it would be fun, plus hopefully another chance to meet some more people in the business with connections.

"Whew! They are so packed tonight!" Lilyanna comments as we scan for an area to sit.

"Look, there's Clint with some of the others. Let's go up there." Ashley points to the balcony above where there are less people but more of the crowd from the Inkers Expo.

A couple hours later, I decide to get some air as I excuse myself from my friends and head outside. I look out over the street below at all people walking around and having fun. Some I know are tourists as they stop every so often to take pictures.

I haven't taken a single moment to do the tourist thing. I'm out of time now since I leave tomorrow. Hopefully I can come again just to visit and look around without worrying about work. I think to myself as I watch everyone below.

"Hey, we all are going to another local spot. Want to come with us?" asks Ashley as she comes up behind me.

"Nah, I think I'll call it a night soon and go back to the hotel. My flight leaves pretty early."

"Have a safe trip and don't forget about all your new friends now." She says with a smile.

I hug her as we say goodbye. Looking back out over the street below I think about all the new connections this week has brought me. I am truly excited to get back home and get started on all the new bookings I have for next week.

As I turn around a guy in the corner catches my eye and I jump a little not expecting to see anyone. *Has he been there the whole time?* I ask myself.

Sneak Peak
Night Howler's MC, Book 1
Reaper's Jewels

Reaper

When a man makes a huge dumbass mistake when it comes to the woman he loves, the best thing he can do is force her back home until she forgives him. Right?

It's not like she is the only one with a reason to be pissed the fuck off. She ran off, had MY kid and was never planning to tell me about her. Yeah, I have a daughter now.

This changes things, it changes everything. I don't give a shit what I have to do, I'll pay every dime that weasel divorce lawyer is trying to get for that bitch I'm married to.

I should have done it three years ago and went after Jade when she left. But I didn't. It was the worst mistake of my life.

Hopefully Jade will forgive me for the last three years. Right now though I think she may want to kill me in my sleep. I didn't give her a choice about going back home.

Jade

He really thinks making me go back to North Mississippi against my will is going to help him win me back. He can go jump off the nearest cliff!

He did want me three years ago. He made that pretty damn plain. Especially when he allowed that bitch to talk to me as if I were just one of the whores that hangs around the club being passed around like a toy.

She had been gone for a couple years and everyone knew Reaper had filed for a divorce. I was so naive to think he was actually in love with me. After what happened that day and the way he acted like she was right about me being nothing to him, I know now, his feelings for me were not that deep.

I have no plans to forgive him. I know he only wants me now because we share a child.

Family means everything to the Star family.

And now our daughter is a part of that.

Buzz

Several years ago, my little sister was raped and murdered. Her killer was never caught. She had been emailing a guy she had met in an online chat room. Even though the authorities had his name he used online, every lead came to a dead end. It didn't stop me from continuing the search.

A few weeks ago I caught a break. Another programmer I knew from when I was still in the service stumbled across the same name with a different unique IP address that constantly bounces around making it almost impossible to follow.

However, follow it I did and where it winds up leading me has me second guessing what I am planning.

I'll take something of his. His beautiful sister Markayla. But we don't hurt innocents. I will protect her as best I can. I plan on her step brother paying for what he did to my sister with his own blood. What I don't plan for is falling hard for my enemy's sister.

Markayla Marie

Even after all of these years I can't believe my mother was stupid enough to fall for my step father. I have never doubted he had something to do with her disappearance. I've just never been able to prove it.

You would think that with her gone, I'd be free of the Marcus family. Unfortunately for me, my step father adopted me when he married my mother.

My step brother absolutely hates me and I am certain that our Papa is the only one keeping him from doing whatever he wanted to me.

The look I see in his eyes any time I run into him while I am out with friends or a date scares me to my core. I refuse to let him know just how scared of him I really am.

If anything ever happens to Papa or I become expendable in his eyes, I will need to run and run fast. Getting away before he gives me to Joe to do whatever he wants with me, will take a miracle.

Chucky's Pride
A Night Howler's MC Story
Maria

Today is my first day back at work in over a month. I took an extended vacation just to get away for a while. The first week on vacation I stayed in Memphis with my best friend Rae. After all the nights spent trying to drink all the Jack Daniels in the area, I am completely surprised my liver is still working properly.

She and I spent most nights partying down on Beale Street, which is where I got my tongue pierced. I had said I was going to do it since my nineteenth birthday several months ago. At first having something like that in your mouth feels really weird, but then you get so used to it, and you forget it's even there. Well, except you find yourself twirling it around in your mouth constantly.

"Good God, I wish you'd stop doing that. It seriously looks like it would hurt," my aunt, and the boss, remarks as I walk in.

We all work in the family owned gas station. It's practically the only one in this little town. Aunt Joy is the manager, my mom is the assistant manager, and I work as a cashier. I have worked here for only about three years, but my mom and Aunt have been here longer.

"It doesn't hurt at all, Aunt Joy. You just don't like seeing it because you are a prude." I add as I stick my tongue out at her causing her to laugh.

"Kaye, can't you do something with your daughter?" she demands of my mom, who is busy stocking the shelves.

"She is twenty years old, Joy. I blame her father for the way that she is."

"You can't blame Daddy, Momma. I spent most of my childhood with you," I smile.

"Why would you get such a thing in your mouth anyway?" my mom asks.

"Because it makes *blowjobs* a little more interesting," I answer as I wag my eyebrows up and down in a suggestive way. My aunt wrinkles her nose and Mom just shakes her head and goes back to stocking the shelves. I just laugh as my Aunt Joy wrinkles her nose at me.

We hear a rumble from outside as a lone rider on a motorcycle pulls up to the gas pumps. From behind the counter, I watch as he gets off the bike and takes his helmet off. All the hair on my arms and neck stand on end as I watch him walk towards the door.

As he steps through the door, his eyes cut my way and just about suck all the air from my body. His blue eyes have me rooted to one spot.

"Bathroom?" he asks.

I vaguely hear my aunt answer his question as I am still standing there like a crazy person watching him stroll to the bathrooms.

My body has never acted like that just from looking at a man. I do have to admit that he is the most gorgeous man I have ever seen. There is just no way he's from around here. They don't grow them like that in Mississippi.

Hell, they don't grow them like that in Tennessee, either. I should know. I just spent most of my vacation there and not once found a guy that even remotely got a second look from me.

A few minutes later, he stands at the counter as I ring up the drinks and snacks he picked out.

I bite my tongue ring, swirling it outside my teeth without even paying attention. "You from around here?" I ask casually.

"I'm from all over really, but currently staying with some of my brothers on the other side of Tupelo. But, I'll be close by here for a few days. Don't know many people around here," he drawls as he looks up at me with a grin.

All I can think is, *Oh, fuck me. He has dimples.* I feel my nipples tightening up against my thin shirt, and I pray he can't see it through it.

"My name is Maria," I grin, "so now you know me. Would you like to get a drink Friday night? I know a really good bar we could go to," I add breathlessly.

"Sounds good to me," he tells me. "Everyone calls me Chucky." He holds his hand out to me palm up, and it takes me a minute to realize he wants my phone.

I watch as he calls himself and hands it back.

"I'll text ya about the details, beautiful." He grins at me as he takes his purchases and backs out the door, staring the whole way.

"Good lord, he sure was pretty. If only I were about thirty years younger," I hear from behind me.

"I thought Maria was going to pass out from the look on her face when she looked at him the first time. She didn't look like she was breathing." My mother jokes to my Aunt.

"She's still not talking, which is strange, should we check her pulse and make sure she is still alive?" asks my Aunt as I turn around to glare at them which doesn't stop them from laughing at my expense.

"Did you at least get his number?" mom finally asks.

"Better than that, I asked him out for a drink this Friday night." I finally smile wide at them both.

"Just don't do anything we wouldn't do." My aunt winks.

"Knowing you two, that doesn't leave a whole lot out." I laugh as they both huff and walk away.

I'll never get tired at riling the two of them up. For one, they make it entirely too easy to do. Even though they both love going out and having a good time, they are both still a little old fashioned about some things.

Connect with the Author

Facebook:
https://www.facebook.com/MarissaAnnAuthor
Instagram:
https://www.instagram.com/authormarissaann/
Twitter:
https://twitter.com/marissaannbooks
Goodreads:
https://www.goodreads.com/author/show/1815985
5.Marissa_Ann

www.ingramcontent.com/pod-product-compliance
Lightning Source LLC
Chambersburg PA
CBHW050147110726
47898CB00008B/2702